A Note to Readers

While the Lankford and Farley families are fictional, the events that happened in Cincinnati during 1832 are not. Cincinnati had one of the worst floods in history and was barely recovering from that disaster when cholera struck.

Dr. Daniel Drake, who befriends Henry and Rachel in this story, is a historical figure. While his theory about "invisible insects" that spread disease was eventually proven wrong, he came very close to discovering germs. His efforts to get people in Cincinnati to clean up the rotting animal carcasses and other garbage in their streets after the flood is credited with saving hundreds of lives. While more than eight hundred people died in Cincinnati during the cholera epidemic of 1832-33, many more lives would have been lost without Dr. Drake's cleanup efforts.

CINCINNATI EPIDEMIC

Veda Boyd Jones

CORBAN UNIVERSITY
LIBRARY
5000 Deer Park Drive SE
Salem, OR 97317-9392

BARBOUR
PUBLISHING, INC.
Uhrichsville, Ohio

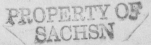

For Morgan, with love

ISBN 1-57748-255-7

Published by Barbour Publishing, Inc.
P.O. Box 719
Uhrichsville, Ohio 44683
www.barbourbooks.com

 Member of the
Evangelical Christian
Publishers Association

Printed in the United States of America.

Cover illustration by Peter Pagano.
Inside illustrations by Adam Wallenta.

CHAPTER 1

The Great Ohio Flood

"River's rising," Henry Lankford told his father. "The men at the wharf say it's up three feet in the last hour. They're moving wagon loads to higher ground." Henry had detoured by the public landing on his way to his father's shipyard, where he was cleanup boy after school.

"We'll go under," Father said matter-of-factly. "I've got three men loading the steam engines. Go on to the toolshed and start loading. I'll send someone else out to help as soon as I can."

Henry ran to the small brick building. He knew the routine from last year, his first year as an extra hand at the yard. The mighty Ohio flooded every spring, but it wasn't usually this early in the year. Even inside the shed he could hear the

5

Ohio's roar. Of course, the shipyard was near the river so that new ships could be launched easily into the water. Sometimes the shipyard went underwater, and sometimes it didn't.

It had rained for two days, but not enough to cause the river to rise this fast. The reach of this flood depended on the amount of rain and melting snow on the western slopes of the Allegheny Mountains. That water fed small streams and the big rivers near Pittsburgh that flowed into the Ohio. Odd that something so far away could affect them here in Cincinnati.

As he filled a wheelbarrow with hammers, wedges, chisels, and saws, Henry was glad for the leather gloves that protected his hands from the cold metal. Once the cart was filled, he pushed it to the main building, where his father was busy loading record books onto a flatbed wagon.

"Where should I take the wheelbarrow?" Henry asked. He glanced toward the rising river water, which was nearing the base of the new sign: Lankford Shipyard. Quality Steamboats. George Lankford, owner. The last sign had been washed away a year ago. But this time, Father had made one that he said should withstand the Ohio's fury. The supports were out of brick, and the sign hung a good twelve feet above ground.

Instead of answering him, Father called to a nearby worker, who helped him lift the wheelbarrow onto the wagon. Father turned to Henry. "Did you get everything?"

"No. Some chains and ropes are still in the shed. I'll go fill another barrow."

Father nodded, and Henry ran toward the shed.

"Wait, Henry."

He turned when he heard Father's voice.

"Go check on the Broadrick sisters and see if they'll go

to our house. Then come right back and load that barrow."

Henry changed directions and ran as quickly as he could toward Plum Street. The cold wind that had been blocked by buildings at the shipyard hit him full force as he dashed down Front Street. At least the downpour had ended at noon, but the sun had never broken through the thick, gray clouds. They looked like snow clouds, which would have been more likely in mid-February than all this rain.

When Henry came to the cross streets, he looked down them toward the river and could see that churning flood-waters now threatened Water Street, which he thought was aptly named. It always went under.

Last spring the Broadrick sisters wouldn't leave their home. They insisted the flood wouldn't reach their home, and they'd been right. But the look and feel of the water was different this year, Henry thought. And it was early.

He pulled his cap lower on his head, leaving only a thatch of blond hair sticking out at the back. As he sprinted along, Henry was bombarded by the sound of men yelling orders, horses neighing as they pulled heavy loads toward higher ground, and women's high-pitched voices as they passed, carrying household items and hustling children away from the river's encroaching waters.

"Raleigh!" Henry called when he saw his friend among the crowd of workers.

"Where are you going?" Raleigh asked. He struggled with a small trunk, half-pulling, half-carrying it. Henry slowed his pace to stay in step with him.

"I'm checking on Miss Hannah and Miss Emma. Who's trunk?"

"I'm helping move Luttman's Mercantile. This is full of

hardware, and it's heavy."

Henry nodded. "I better run. I've got to get back and help Father as soon as I see if they're all right. Think it will get high?"

"Higher than a kite," Raleigh said.

Henry bolted off and was out of breath by the time he reached Plum Street. He was sweating under his heavy coat, but he could see his breath in the frigid air.

He knocked on the door of the two-story brick house and hollered, "Miss Emma!"

A moment later Miss Emma Broadrick opened the door. "Hello, Henry. Come in."

He stepped inside the hall so the winter air wouldn't enter the house. "I've got to get back to the shipyard. Father sent me to ask you to go to our house. The water's bound to reach your home this year."

"Now, Henry, I've seen a few more floods than you have," Miss Emma said with a laugh. She always laughed after she said something—an odd habit, Henry thought. "The water won't get this high."

"We're moving the engines and machinery," Henry said in an effort to convince her.

"We're moving some of our belongings upstairs, just in case," she said. "Hannah insists, but I don't think we're in any danger."

Henry glanced down the hall to the parlor. Although furniture was still in place, lamps and some of Miss Emma's decorative figurines were missing.

Miss Hannah's frail figure appeared at the top of the stairs, and she slowly made her way down by holding onto the railing.

"Are you here to help us take things upstairs?" she asked. She was the elder of the two sisters, and Henry guessed her age to be nearing seventy.

"We could use the help," Miss Emma added. She was at least five years younger than her sister, although she looked younger than that, probably because she got around so much better. She also weighed twice what her sister weighed and had that loud laugh.

Henry silently groaned. "For a few minutes," he said. "Father's expecting me back at the yard." But wouldn't his father also expect him to help the Broadrick sisters? They ate Sunday dinner with the Lankfords nearly every week after church, and Henry's father had known them since long before Henry had been born.

As quickly as he could, Henry climbed the stairs, loaded down with foodstuff and kitchen utensils. He made several trips, carrying chairs and small tables. Then he helped Miss Emma carry the heavy dining room table.

"You'll come back tomorrow and help us carry all this back down, won't you?" Miss Emma asked.

"Yes, ma'am," Henry answered.

"It won't be tomorrow," Miss Hannah said. "The river's taking control."

Henry grabbed the opportunity, since Miss Hannah obviously agreed with his opinion of the flood. "Then why don't you go to our house, where you'll be out of the river's reach?" he asked.

"Oh, we couldn't leave Papa's house," Miss Hannah said. "We'll be fine."

Henry glanced at the mantle clock as he grabbed it and carried it upstairs. His few minutes of helping had turned into an hour already. Father would be wondering where he was. But could he leave these women carrying their treasures upstairs? Miss Hannah made one trip for every six of his. Miss Emma lumbered up and down twice as fast as her sister, but still painstakingly slow. Making the decision to stay and help, Henry asked, "What else do you want carried upstairs?"

"What about that trunk of Mama's in the back room?" Miss Hannah asked.

"Oh, yes, we'll need that upstairs," Miss Emma agreed, and Henry hurried to fetch the trunk. It was one of the few times he'd heard the two sisters agree on anything.

After another dozen trips up the stairs, Henry heard commotion outside. Earlier there had been the noise of people hurrying by, carrying boxes or driving teams of horses, but this was different.

"It's surging," he heard someone call.

He raced to the window and saw muddy river water rushing toward them. Both women were upstairs, and he took the stairs two at a time.

"It's coming," he yelled.

The sisters were already at the bedroom window, looking down on the street below.

"It can't get this high," Miss Emma said. "It might get in the cellar, but this house is built too far off the ground to be in any danger."

Henry didn't want to argue with the woman, but panic was building inside him. He was doing everything in his power not to scream.

"Dear God, help us be safe," Miss Hannah prayed, and Henry added his "Amen" in a high voice he barely recognized as his own.

"Run down and get some firewood," Miss Emma ordered him. "The wood box in the kitchen is full."

Henry didn't want to leave the scene at the window, but he did as he was told. He made two trips with his arms full of wood before water seeped in under the front door. On his third trip to the kitchen, he was wading in inch-deep water. He'd just started his fourth trip up the stairs when he heard a crash. An instant later the front door burst open. River water gushed through. A log, carried by the great force of the current, had rammed against the door, breaking the lock.

Henry dropped his load of firewood and flew up the stairs, yelling for the sisters.

"What was that noise?" Miss Emma asked as she met him at the top of the stairs.

Henry stood paralyzed, looking down at the swirling water and the big log that now blocked part of the doorway.

"Oh, no," she said.

The water lapped at the staircase about a third of the way to the top. Firewood floated and bumped time and again against the walls.

"Let's get inside the front bedroom," she said.

Somehow Henry forced himself to walk the few steps down the hall to the room. Miss Hannah's pale face stared at him, then she turned back to the window.

"I knew it would come in this time," she said. "It hasn't flooded like this for thirty years, but I knew this time the river would take over."

"Well, it won't get this high," Miss Emma said. She added a piece of wood to the fireplace, and Henry shivered when he saw the orange-colored flames lick around the wood. The room was damp and cold now that the downstairs was open to the winter cold and the icy river.

"I left the door open at the top of the stairs," Miss Emma said. "I forgot to shut it."

Without waiting for another order from the big woman, Henry walked to the bedroom door and slipped out into the hall. The water now reached halfway up the stairs. With a deft movement, he closed the stairwell door and prayed that the water wouldn't get high enough to shove it open.

He wondered if Father had gotten his equipment to higher ground. And he wondered if Mother and Louisa were safe at home and if they worried about where he was.

"I've shut it," he said when he returned.

"Take off your shoes and stockings and put these on," Miss Emma directed. She held out some women's stockings, but he didn't care. His feet were numb with the cold.

With his shoes and stockings drying by the fire, Henry padded over to the window where Miss Hannah kept watch.

"Be night soon," she said.

Dusk was already falling as the gray sky became darker and rain once again fell. The street below took on an unreal appearance. Henry had never seen Plum Street underwater. From his vantage point at the high window, he could see to Water Street and beyond to the channel of the mighty Ohio. Other two-story houses across the street looked like one-story houses.

"It sure came up fast," Henry said.

"The current must have built up a dam of logs and brush downriver, then broken through," Miss Hannah said. "That's happened before."

"Look," Miss Emma said in an awed voice and tapped on the window glass. "Must be from the shantytown."

In the distance Henry could see a frame house being swept down the churning rapids. Could the powerful Ohio destroy the Broadricks' house, too?

CHAPTER 2

The Waters Recede

"Don't worry," Miss Hannah said. "Papa made this house good and strong. The Ohio won't move one brick of it."

Oddly enough, Henry believed her. Or was he still in shock? For the last half hour, every time he'd looked outside, he'd gasped at the sight. Now it was too dark to see anything but his reflection in the window.

Miss Emma had lit a lantern and had settled her big mass in front of the fireplace. She tended cheese, which she was toasting over the flames. When it browned and started to melt, she placed it on thick slices of bread.

"My father—" Henry started.

"George can't get here until daylight, if then," Miss Emma said. "The current may still be too strong. You might as well settle down for the evening. Here's our dinner."

"There's only been one other time it's gotten in the house," Miss Hannah said. "That was when Papa hung the hook in the fireplace, just in case it happened again. We were up here for two weeks until the water went down. We had soup every day. You should have thought of water, Emma."

"I should have thought of it! I was toting your keepsakes up the stairs. You should have thought of it," Miss Emma said with a laugh. "We both should have thought of it."

Two weeks. Henry couldn't stay two weeks with the Broadrick sisters. Surely Father would come for him at first light.

"Shall I say grace?" Miss Emma asked.

"I'll say it," Miss Hannah said and launched into a long prayer of thankfulness that they were all alive and well.

"Amen," Henry said. He ate his bread and cheese and immediately felt thirsty, but there was no drinkable water. All he had to do was step down a few stairs and he could get them all the water they'd need, but it was filthy water, and it smelled of outhouses and garbage.

There was little to do but visit with Miss Hannah and Miss Emma without taking sides on every issue they debated. He had always liked both women, but they had different opinions about everything they talked about. They weren't mean about it, they just disagreed.

The night wore on. Henry curled up in a heavy quilt near the fire. Noises downstairs woke him several times. Probably debris banging against the walls or the furniture they hadn't carried upstairs floating into the staircase. Miss Emma snored, which was almost as loud as her laugh.

The rain stopped early in the night, and, once, Henry got up to look outside. The clouds had moved on. Stars twinkled above, and moonlight reflected off the water. The churning and swirling action that he'd seen earlier was gone, and the water gurgled between the houses. He fed the fire a couple sticks of firewood and settled back on the floor.

"Henry! Henry!"

He was startled awake at daybreak and rushed to the window and pushed it open.

"Father!"

"Thank the good Lord, you're safe." Henry could hear the relief in Father's voice. "I knew you'd be here. I knew you would be."

The two sisters crowded at the window.

"Good morning, George," Miss Emma said and laughed. "Come to take your son home?"

"I suspect he's overstayed his welcome," Father said.

"Oh, he was a big help to us yesterday evening," Miss Hannah said and related the story of moving their belongings upstairs in infinite detail.

While she was talking, Henry put on his dry stockings and shoes and walked to the top of the stairs. He was almost afraid to open the door, but curiosity overcame his fear. The floodwater had risen to four steps below the second floor. He quickly shut the door again.

The bedroom was cold from the opened window, so Henry slipped on his coat and put more logs on the fire. Now that it was time to go, he was having second thoughts. Could the sisters manage without him here? Or could he get them out the window to the boat?

He couldn't picture Miss Hannah having the strength to hold onto a rope, and Miss Emma might break it.

"Henry?"

16

He scurried to the window.

"I'll throw this up, and you can tie it to something that will hold."

Obviously Father thought he could leave the two sisters. Henry caught the rope on the first throw and tied it to the bedpost.

"Will you be all right here?" he asked Miss Hannah.

"We'll be fine if you keep us supplied with water and firewood," Miss Emma answered. "And maybe some food, too," she added and laughed.

"I'll bring you supplies every day," Henry promised. "Thank you for dinner last night," he added politely. Then with relief he reached for the rope.

Climbing out the window and holding onto the rope at the same time was no easy feat. The sisters could never have done it. Henry struggled to wrap his legs around the rope and lower himself hand-over-hand. Father held the other end of the rope and guided Henry's feet to the hardwood flooring of the rowboat. Once he'd untangled himself, Henry grabbed his father, and they hugged each other tight.

"Thank God you're all right," Father said again. "Let's tell your mother you're safe, and then we'll bring the Broadricks some water."

"It's got to be ten feet deep here," Henry told Rachel Farley as their rowboat floated down Elm Street. The shingle that jutted out over Luttman's Mercantile was almost that high off the street, and only the tip of it was above the water. He could reach out and touch it if he tried.

"I can't believe it's so deep," Rachel said. She was Henry's cousin, a few times removed. Their families jokingly called each other distant cousins because Rachel's family lived on a farm outside of town and Henry's lived smack inside Cincinnati, but on higher ground than the flooded downtown area. "Are we near the Broadricks' house?" she asked.

"Almost," Henry said. A light snow started as he turned the boat onto Front Street. A couple minutes later, he slowed the boat as they reached the sisters' dwelling on Plum.

"Ahoy," Henry shouted, and the Broadrick sisters waved from the second-floor window.

"What have you brought us today?" Miss Emma called once she'd opened the window.

"Fresh eggs," Henry answered. "Lower the rope." He caught the free end and tied it to the water pail. Miss Emma pulled the pail up. Henry rocked the boat as he crawled toward the bow. Yesterday Miss Emma had spilled a good portion of the water, and it had splashed on him. He wasn't going to risk that again. His cap and coat were already getting wet from the snow.

"Is that Rachel with you?" Miss Emma asked as she lowered the now empty pail.

"Yes, Miss Emma," Rachel answered.

"She brought the eggs and milk in from the farm," Henry said, untying the rope and knotting it around the basket of food that Rachel held. Once again Miss Emma pulled up the rope.

"Tie on the wood rug," Henry said, and once it was lowered, he filled it with firewood. "Do you need anything else today?"

"No, we'll be fine until tomorrow," Miss Emma said. "Thank you."

"See you then," Henry said and paddled the boat through the snow toward Main Street.

"God bless you," Miss Hannah called after them.

"I wouldn't want to be stuck on the second floor like that," Rachel said. "It would be like living on a deserted island."

"Except they're not really alone. They see me and others from church every day," Henry said. "Father says this could last a couple weeks, and I'm in charge of taking them supplies." This was the second day that Henry had been allowed to take the boat out on his own. At first the water had been too swift, but now that it was starting to recede, Father had turned responsibility for the Broadrick sisters' care over to Henry.

"It's weird seeing snow on water," Rachel said. "It doesn't stick."

Henry nodded. It was odd seeing snow disappear instead of building up. He was almost eleven, and he'd never seen it snow on this much water. Most winters while the snow fell, he didn't venture out very far—to school and home, but not to the docks on the river.

Henry guided the boat through the whirl of white toward what was normally a busy wharf area. "The flooded area's about a mile wide. That's a powerful lot of water to get downstream."

"Look there!" Rachel exclaimed. At the public landing, three steamboats were tied to trees because the wharves were underwater.

"Father says there's too much debris in the water to travel, even for a steamship. See how fast the water's moving out in the channel?"

The cousins explored the flooded streets, with Henry occasionally calling out for any other stranded townspeople. No one answered. The eerie quiet was in stark contrast to five days earlier, when shouting merchants, with every hand they could find, had been moving their goods to upper floors or higher ground.

"Look there!" Rachel said again. Water poured into the fourth story of the steam mill, counting down from the top. "How deep do you think the river is?"

"Maybe seventy feet in the channel," Henry said, parroting what he'd heard his father discuss with the men of the families who were staying with them until they could return to their flooded homes. "Have you seen enough? We ought to be getting home. Aunt Betsy might be waiting on you to start back to the farm." Rachel's mother wasn't really his aunt, but that's what he called her.

"I'm sure glad Mama let me come today. Our creek is up, but it's nothing like this."

"Father says the flood of '32 will be remembered for a long time."

"It's the worst I've ever seen. But why do you live here and get flooded year after year? That makes no sense," Rachel said.

"Father can't build steamships and carry them to the river," Henry said defensively. "His yard has to be on the water."

Rachel shrugged. "I'd never live here. It floods *every* year. It's never missed one year."

"We're used to it," Henry said. "And nobody was drowned this year."

"Thank God for that," Rachel said.

He couldn't argue with her on that point, so he gave his energy to rowing the boat back toward home. When they got to the edge of the floodwaters, he jumped onto a sidewalk and tied the boat to a hitching post. He held the skiff steady while Rachel climbed out, holding her skirts up so the hem wouldn't get wet and muddy. Henry carried the empty water pail, and Rachel carried the basket on the quarter-mile walk to the Lankford house.

The place was bursting with activity. Aunt Betsy and Uncle Andrew, plus Rachel's little brother and sister, Henry's sister and parents, and the two extra families filled the house with noise.

Rachel described the flooded area to her mother.

"George," Aunt Betsy said to Henry's father, "do you remember the big flood a few days after we moved to Cincinnati? We were scared to death we couldn't get all our belongings moved out of the warehouse before the Ohio ruined them."

"I remember," Father said. "You saved my dog."

"That Jefferson was a pesky animal," Betsy said. "And I think your new dog might be just like him." She motioned to the window where Henry's little brown dog was whining to get inside.

Father grinned. "We call him Jackson."

"Why do you name your dogs after presidents?" Betsy asked.

"Reminds me who's in office," he said and laughed.

The grown-ups talked a few more minutes before Rachel's parents rounded up their children. Henry stood on the porch with the others while Rachel's father hitched the team to the wagon. Then they loaded empty egg baskets and milk containers.

"We'll bring more goods into town on market day," Aunt Betsy said.

"Thanks for showing me the flood," Rachel called to Henry. "Wait till I tell my friends at school. They won't believe it."

Henry found it hard to believe, too. Within a week, the excitement of having extra people around had worn off. Everyone got crankier and crankier as the water slowly receded.

School, which Henry loved and where he excelled, had been called off because homeless people were living there until the water went down and they could reclaim their homes—if their homes were still there.

Every day Henry delivered supplies to the Broadricks, and every day the walk to the boat got longer as the water receded. Now he could see through the Broadricks' opened front door that the water in the parlor stood about three feet deep. It took a longer rope to reach the water bucket. And the longer the rope, the more water Miss Emma spilled on Henry.

Rachel came back to town on market day with her family. They lived seven miles out of town. Although her father brought goods to market, Rachel didn't always come mid-week during the school session. But she always came on Saturdays, and in the summers she came in on Wednesday, too. Once again Henry took her on his route to the Broadricks.

"It smells awful," Rachel said.

"You get used to it," Henry defended his town. He still gagged sometimes, but he didn't like her saying anything about it.

After he'd made his delivery to the Broadrick sisters, he rowed over to the public landing.

"The steamboats are gone," Rachel said.

"They've been running for several days now. Some will dock here later this afternoon." He maneuvered the rowboat to avoid a roof sticking out of the water. It was all that was left of a house that had finally caved in.

"You can see more floors of the steam mill," Henry pointed out.

"This place is a mess," Rachel said. "It's going to take years to get all this cleaned up." She made a gesture with her hands that encompassed the entire downtown. "It might not be cleaned up in time for next year's flood. Our creek is already flowing normally." She made it sound like the country was more in charge of nature than the city was.

"It'll be hard work, but we'll get it cleaned up," Henry said. He wound up the tour and took Rachel back to his house, where Aunt Betsy and her two other children were waiting.

He was glad to see their wagon pull away from the house. Usually he could take Rachel's outspokenness and even liked arguing with her. He was pleased that he could hold his own against her.

Rachel was eleven, almost twelve, a year older than he was, but now he was a reader ahead of her in school. And he'd worked hard to get put ahead. If there was one thing Henry loved to do, it was read. He had read nearly every book in the school and quite a few that he had gotten from the public library. The more he read, the more his teacher had given him to read.

"Reading is the basis of knowledge," the headmaster had said. "The more you read, the more you know. The more you know, the more you'll get out of life."

And Henry had agreed with the teacher. He had traveled to faraway places in his reading, but he still appreciated Cincinnati best. He had also worked all sorts of problems in arithmetic. On his own, he had added up all the chapters in every book in the Bible, and he had figured out if he read five chapters a day, he could read the entire Bible in one year. He was already halfway through the Old Testament.

He liked discussing religion with Rachel, too, and he usually knew more about the Bible than she did.

By the next market day, when he saw Rachel again, the floodwaters had gone down fast. It was as if someone had knocked a big hole in a washtub, and *whoosh,* the water was gone. And what was left! If the place had the stench of sewer and stagnant water before, now it was worse than ever.

Rachel agreed to help Henry hand-carry supplies to the Broadrick sisters. He wore a bandanna sprinkled with cinnamon oil around his neck to pull up over his nose when the smell got too bad. He handed one to Rachel.

She tied it on, and they started toward the Broadricks'. As long as they were on the high store sidewalks, which were covered with sand and silt, Rachel was willing to go. But once they had to cross the street, she balked.

Driftwood littered the streets, but that was the least of the problems. It could easily be carted away and burned. Caught among piles of broken lumber were the swollen bodies of dead pigs. Before the flood, they had prowled the streets and ate the garbage of the town. Now the dead ones stank and were covered with maggots.

"I'm not going in that filth," Rachel said.

"You've got to," Henry said. "I can't carry all this alone."

Rachel set her basket and water pail on the sidewalk. "Then you can make a trip back here and get it. I'm not going one more step."

"Fine." Defiantly, Henry stepped off the sidewalk and sank knee-deep in mud and slime.

CHAPTER 3
The Snakes

"I should never have told Mama that I didn't go with you," Rachel said as she and Henry walked down Elm Street toward the Broadrick sisters' home. They both carried pails of water, and Henry carried a bag of lye soap and some scrub brushes from the shipyard.

As angry as he'd been when Rachel had refused to deliver food the other day, he was equally glad that on this trip she had to help him with the cleanup at the Broadricks'.

The streets were passable, but only a lane wide enough for a wagon had been cleared of the silt and debris. Merchants were cleaning out their stores, but it was slow work, and great mounds of sand and mud swelled in front of the businesses. Henry and Rachel stayed in the lane when they could and dodged two fires in the middle of cross streets where the carcasses of dead pigs were being burned. The stench was horrible.

Finally they turned onto Plum Street. The Broadricks' front door was still open. It was impossible to shut. The river had deposited sand, silt, and mud six inches deep, and although for two days Henry had shoveled out tons of sludge, there was still more. Father had come over last night after he'd worked at the shipyard cleanup and shoveled even more out. The sludge was piled in front of the house, but Father said they'd shovel it onto a wagon and take it to the low marshy area on the edge of town whenever he had free time and an extra wagon. Right now his equipment was in use at the shipyard.

"Good morning," Henry called. Miss Emma opened the door at the head of the stairs.

"Good morning, Henry. I'm glad to see you brought fresh drinking water."

"Yes, ma'am. And I brought Rachel to help us, too."

"Many hands make light work," she said and laughed that loud laugh.

"Where do you want me to start?" Rachel asked in a voice that said this was a hopeless task.

"We've got the sludge out of the kitchen," Henry said. "You can start scrubbing the walls in there."

With a heavy sigh, Rachel went into the kitchen. Henry carried the water pails upstairs and then returned to the kitchen.

It didn't look too bad. He'd even gotten the cookstove cleaned out the day before. Of course, it needed a good scrubbing, but by nightfall the sisters might use it to prepare their evening meal. The place still smelled to high heaven, but that wasn't going to change anytime soon. The musty, stinky odor would probably linger until the Fourth of July.

Henry left Rachel and Miss Emma and started shoveling in the parlor, where he'd left off. His shoulders ached from the last two days of work. The hill outside the door grew larger and larger as he scooped and shoved and scraped the goo off the floor.

A loud scream from the kitchen froze his blood.

"Leave it alone," Rachel yelled.

Henry dropped the shovel, raced to the kitchen, and nearly collided with Miss Emma.

The upstairs door banged open. "What's wrong?" Miss Hannah called.

"A snake," Miss Emma screamed.

"It's not poisonous," Rachel said. "It's a harmless water snake." She was poking the end of the broom into a cupboard. "Maybe I can get it outside."

"Kill it, Henry!" Miss Emma squealed.

"It isn't hurting anything," Rachel said. "I'll get it out. Do you have a bag we can put it in? I'll take it to the river."

"Kill it!" Miss Emma demanded in a stronger voice.

"There's no need to kill anything," Miss Hannah declared, standing in the kitchen doorway. "That's an innocent snake."

"If I had a flour sack, I could put the snake inside and take it to the river," Rachel said over her shoulder. She had not taken her eyes off the snake, which had now coiled around the broom handle.

"There's one in this cupboard," Miss Hannah said. She made her way to another cupboard and tried to open the door. "It's swollen shut. Henry?"

Henry pried the door open and took out a soggy, stinky bag. He held the sides out so that Rachel could stick the end of the broom handle in it and force the snake off. It wasn't something he wanted to do, but he wasn't going to act like he was afraid of a water snake in front of Rachel.

Once the snake dropped into the bag, Henry twisted the top, and Miss Hannah handed him a piece of twine she had gotten from the cupboard. Henry took the snake bag out the back door and laid it on the step. He and Rachel could take it to the river when they left.

"Why don't you clean that stove up so we can have a fire?" Miss Hannah said. It was obvious she was used to being in charge. "Heat would help dry this place out. What about the fireplace in the parlor, Henry? Can you build a fire in there yet?"

Henry couldn't believe he hadn't thought of that. March meant spring, but it sure didn't feel like spring yet. He'd been shoveling with his coat on, which hindered his movements and slowed him down.

"I'll get right to it." He hurried out to the new woodpile and picked up an armful of wood and some lighter twigs for kindling. Father had brought wood yesterday, and other members of their church congregation had also brought firewood to replenish the Broadrick sisters' supply.

He spent a few minutes wiping off the hearth and the wooden mantle before he started a fire. Soon the snap and crackle of little twigs told him the fire was burning, but it took some time and a lot of smoke up the chimney before some of the larger, damp pieces of wood caught fire.

Henry had started shoveling again when he glanced back at the fireplace and saw not one, but two snakes slither down the bricks. He couldn't hold back a startled screech.

"Rachel, bring your broom," he shouted.

She raced into the room.

"Two more. They must have been on the smoke shelf in the chimney."

The snakes had crawled to a corner and curled up side by side. Henry ran for the snake sack.

"What is it?" Miss Emma asked from the floor, where her large bulk was hunched in front of the cookstove.

"Another snake," Henry said, feeling it was better to tell a half-truth than mention that there were two. "It was in the chimney," he added quickly. "They go for closed-in spaces, so I'm sure that's the last one."

Miss Emma's eyes got bigger, if that were possible, as she glanced at the compartments in the stove she was cleaning.

"We'll look in all the small areas as soon as we get these out," Henry said and opened the back door to fetch the snake bag. The captured one wiggled when he picked up the bag, and he almost dropped it.

He ran back into the parlor and watched as Rachel expertly poked at one snake until it wrapped around the broom handle.

"How do you know how to do that?" he asked.

"We have snakes at the creek. They're sluggish this time of year or they'd probably be slithering all over this place instead of staying in the corner."

"Why aren't you afraid of them like most girls?" Henry asked.

"They're just animals, like rabbits or dogs," she said in a low voice.

Before he untied the twine, Henry shook the snake down

to the bottom of the flour sack, then held it open so Rachel could drop the second snake inside. He repeated the same procedure for the third snake, then quickly retied the twine.

"I told Miss Emma we'd look in other tight places for any other snakes."

He was glad they'd carried so much furniture upstairs, but there was still a buffet in the dining room. Gingerly, he and Rachel looked through the filthy tablecloths and doilies that were stored there, but they found no other snakes.

"These linens need to be washed, and we need to carry this buffet outside so it can dry in the sun," Rachel said.

They wrestled the thing between them and got it out in the backyard. Miss Hannah came down and said she'd stir the linen in the washtub if Henry would draw water from the well. He lowered the bucket, then pulled it up. The water was a little murky, but it was okay for the laundry, Miss Hannah decided.

By lunchtime Henry had hung out the washing, started a fire in the cookstove, and finished shoveling out the parlor. As soon as the group ate a bowl of soup upstairs in the bedroom, Henry and Rachel returned downstairs to work while the sisters took a brief rest.

"We always lie down after lunch," Miss Emma said. "At our age, it's necessary."

Henry had never thought about needing a nap, but he thought he could use a little shut-eye himself after putting in a hard morning's work. He wanted to go to sleep and forget the flood had ever happened. He could close his eyes and make this sludge that covered the floors, the streets, and the yards disappear. But that wouldn't make life return to normal and let him go back to school.

"What about the cellar?" Rachel asked when the two of them were back downstairs. Her words effectively brought him away from his daydream and back to the reality of flood cleanup.

"We haven't looked," Henry said. "There's a door over there." He pointed to a narrow door near the stove.

Rachel opened the door, and Henry looked past her to the darkness below.

"We'll need a lamp," she said.

Henry lit the lamp he'd brought downstairs last night when Father had shoveled out the sludge. He carried it to the head of the narrow stairs, but it did little to illuminate the blackness of the cellar. One step down, two, then three. On the fourth one, he stepped into water. He backed up one step and stooped down, holding the lamp in front of him.

"There's still water down here," he said. And there was something in the water. Circles showed that something had surfaced, then submerged again. He hoped it was a fish, but something told him it wasn't. "And something else. Come look at this," he said.

Rachel squeezed close beside him.

"More snakes?" she asked.

"I think so." He held the lamp out as far as his arm would reach, and this time he saw a snake's head, its two eyes yellow in the lamplight. He almost dropped the lamp. He grabbed it with his free hand and would have lost his balance if Rachel hadn't pulled him back. "Let's close this door."

They lost no time climbing back up the few steps to the kitchen, and Henry shut the cellar door.

"You can't catch that one with the broomstick, can you?"

"No, and that gap's big enough for it to come right

31

through," Rachel said, "but I think it'll stay down there."

Just the same, Henry grabbed the rag Miss Emma had used to clean the stove and stuffed it at the bottom of the door.

"We can't tell them," he said. "They've been living with snakes here all this time. There's nothing we can do except scare them."

"Or at least scare Miss Emma," Rachel said. "Miss Hannah seems able to stand anything."

Henry nodded. Odd. Miss Emma was certainly the stronger-bodied of the two, but Miss Hannah was stronger when it came to taking things in stride.

"This room is looking good," he said. "I'll get back to the dining room." It was the last room to scrape out. He'd almost welcome Rachel's job, scrubbing the walls and cupboards with lye soap. At least the smell would be different.

By late afternoon, Henry and Rachel had put in a full day's work. Miss Emma had come back downstairs, but her sister stayed upstairs.

"What a difference this day has made," she said. "We can cook supper down here. I can bake bread tomorrow."

"Except Mother told me to ask you to Sunday dinner," Henry said. "And she said she won't take excuses. She said that it was time you two got out of this house, and Father will pick you up at the usual time for church."

"Then we'll be waiting for him," Miss Emma said with a laugh. "I'll bake bread on Monday. You'll be back then, won't you, Henry?"

"Yes, ma'am," he said.

"You, too, Rachel?"

"No, I'll be in school. But I may be back on market day. I'll ask Mama."

Miss Emma thanked them for their help and reminded them to take the snake bag off the back porch.

Henry stuck the bag in one of the water pails, and he and Rachel carried it to the river, just a few blocks away. Henry carefully untied the sack, then shook it upside down. The snakes plopped into the water. He watched them swim away.

"If you hadn't been there today, I would have killed them," he said.

"Then I'm glad I was there," Rachel said, "although I'm tired and ready to go back to the farm. Cleaning up after this flood is hard work."

They started back toward Henry's house, again dodging huge piles of sludge.

"Look around," Rachel said. "This will take years to clean up. Where are they going to put all this stinky stuff? They can't leave it here on the streets."

"Father's going to a meeting about it tonight at Dr. Drake's house," Henry said. "They'll decide how to get rid of it."

"Still, it'll take years," Rachel said. "How can you stand living here in all this?"

He didn't want to argue with her. Today they had gotten along pretty well. She had agreed with him about keeping the cellar snake a secret from the sisters, and she had worked hard. And although he loved Cincinnati, he was tired of the mess, too.

"Father and Dr. Drake will know what to do" was all he said. "It'll get better."

But later that night, when Father returned from Dr. Drake's home, Henry learned that it could get worse.

"Dr. Drake says cholera is in England. It'll reach the East Coast this summer. He's sure of it. And he says it's just a matter of time before it will come here."

"What's cholera?" Henry asked.

"It's a disease that can kill people in hours. Someone can get it in the morning and be dead by night. It's all in these magazines Dr. Drake loaned me." Father thumbed his hand against a couple publications. "And Dr. Drake says it's coming here. He doesn't know when, but it's coming here."

Chapter 4
Henry's Opportunity

On Sunday morning Henry went with Father in the wagon to give the Broadrick sisters a ride to church. Henry hadn't told anyone about the snake in the cellar, and the omission weighed on him. He'd even lied when he told Miss Emma there was one snake in the chimney when there were two.

It didn't help his conscience any that the sermon was about the Ten Commandments. It seemed to Henry that the preacher shouted extra loud when he got to the commandment about lying. He squirmed on the hard bench and looked down at the floor.

"If we all lived by the Golden Rule, we would have no quarrel with our neighbor," Preacher Tierney said. "We would have no problems in Cincinnati over the flood cleanup. Everyone would help his neighbor in the same way that he would want to be helped if his own house had flooded. We all use the streets. Shouldn't we all help clean them up? We should help our neighbors; we should help our friends; we should help our enemies."

While the preacher talked about enemies for a while, Henry didn't listen. He turned his thoughts back to the Golden Rule. He was helping his friends with their house. It was true, Mother and Father had told him to do it, but he was willingly helping. Did that make up for the lying? Or was that following the Golden Rule, too? If he were living in a house that had a snake in the cellar, would he want to know?

If there was nothing he could do about it until the water went down, he wouldn't want to worry about it. Because he would worry. He didn't like snakes. It had taken every bit of strength he had in him not to flinch while he held that bag open for Rachel. And Miss Emma was more afraid of snakes than he was, although the snakes didn't seem to bother Miss Hannah.

Miss Hannah. He would confess to her, and she could decide whether to tell Miss Emma or not. Was it lying if he were doing it for her own good?

His attention returned to the preacher when he heard a collective gasp from the congregation.

"Dr. Daniel Drake has told me that cholera breeds in filthy places, and our recently flooded areas are perfect places for it. He urges everyone to dispose of the sludge in the middle of the river. If it's dumped at the edge, it could wash back up on the banks.

"If we obey the Golden Rule, we'll all help each other get Cincinnati back to normal and lessen the effect cholera has on our town."

After the sermon, church members buzzed with talk of

cholera. Henry heard one man say that cholera could kill someone in a matter of minutes. Surely that wasn't so. He had to get his hands on those magazines that Dr. Drake had lent to Father.

As promised, the Broadrick sisters joined Henry's family for Sunday dinner. Talk centered on the cleanup and the cholera epidemic in Europe. Henry asked for permission to read Dr. Drake's magazines, and Father said he didn't think that would hurt a thing.

It was after dinner before Henry had a chance to speak with Miss Hannah alone. He helped her to the parlor and made sure the others had gone in ahead. Once he told her about the two snakes in the chimney and the one in the water, she stared at him a moment before she spoke.

"Well, Henry, Emma didn't ask you directly if there were any more snakes, so I reckon you did the right thing in not volunteering the information. But you also did the right thing in telling me. Now I can be on the lookout, but not let on to Emma."

A load lifted off Henry's shoulders just as sure as if God had lifted a ten-pound harness from him.

"Now give me your arm to lean on so we can join the others," Miss Hannah said and smiled at him. "You've sure been good help to us with this flood. I knew it was going to be a big one."

While the adults talked, Henry sat in his loft bedroom by the window and read Dr. Drake's magazines. Father and Dr. Drake had been friends since Father was a boy. He had told Henry about the winter of the earthquakes and how Dr. Drake had shown him how to set up pendulums so he'd know when an earthquake was coming, although most of them came in the night, when he wasn't near his pendulums. According to Father, Dr. Drake was always doing experiments.

Now Henry looked at the medical magazines that were full of news from Europe about the cholera epidemic. Different doctors wrote about their views on how the disease spread. He'd have to ask Dr. Drake for his opinion. Henry didn't understand the technical words, but he got the gist of the articles, and he was full of questions.

Henry's father also read the magazines, and he and Henry discussed the disease.

"You'll have to go with me to return these to Dr. Drake," Father said. "Then you can ask your questions."

But it was several days before they had an opportunity. Their friends who had been staying with them had finally gotten their homes clean enough to move back into, so Mother and Louisa helped Henry at the Broadricks'. And on market day, Rachel returned to town and volunteered to help with the final day of scrubbing.

Henry and Rachel checked the cellar, but the ground beneath it was so saturated, it couldn't absorb water very fast. The water had only gone down a foot.

Mother joined the discussion at the cellar door. "We'll never get this place smelling better if we don't get rid of that water and all those rotting vegetables down there. Henry, take a pail to the outside cellar door and dip that water out. The place won't dry if we don't. And according to what Dr. Drake told Father, that's where cholera can breed."

That word brought fear to Henry's heart. He hadn't seen anywhere in those magazines about people dying in minutes of getting the disease. And he didn't know how people caught it. The articles said it was not contagious, so it couldn't spread from one person to the next. So, why did they say it was coming to Cincinnati if it wasn't carried by someone? It didn't make sense.

"Should we dump the water in the backyard?" he asked. He didn't see how it could hurt. They still had mounds of sludge everywhere. As soon as Father finished at the shipyard, he said he'd bring the wagon and some men over and they'd take that stuff to the middle of the river, like Dr. Drake suggested.

"Just dump it away from the house," Mother said.

Rachel carried a bucket outside, too. Henry lifted the heavy cellar door and propped it open. Water reached to the top step, so Henry stood in the yard and dipped his pail in. He handed it to Rachel, and she emptied it a few yards away, where the sun had dried out the mud, while Henry filled the second bucket.

"Watch for that snake," Rachel warned him.

"I am," Henry said. The snake had been at the front of his mind, but he hadn't seen it so far.

After awhile they traded positions, and Rachel dipped and Henry carried the water off to empty it. The cellar wasn't a large area—maybe six feet long by four feet wide—but it held a lot of water. After an hour of dipping, they had only lowered the water by half, and the backyard was looking like it had been flooded again.

"Maybe we ought to let the water sink in the ground before we do any more of this," Rachel said, and Henry agreed.

"You two have been working hard," Mother said when Henry reported for another job. In the scrape-out phase, he had known what to do. Now that they were washing curtains and such, he was glad to have Mother in charge. "Would you take those magazines back to Dr. Drake? Your father meant to do it last night, but it got too late, so I told him I'd take them today, before we went back home."

Henry took the magazines from the mantle, where Mother had put them out of harm's way, and he and Rachel fairly skipped out the front door.

"My arm's about to fall off," Rachel said. "Those water pails are heavy."

It wasn't far from Plum Street to Dr. Drake's house on Vine, and they found him on the front porch as he was about to leave to check on some patients.

Henry was normally not bashful, but he always found himself attacked by shyness when he was with the renowned doctor. He introduced Rachel and handed the magazines to Dr. Drake. "Father says thank you for letting him read them."

"What did he think?" Dr. Drake asked.

"He said we should all be working together to clean up the flood areas before the cholera gets here." This was Henry's opportunity, and he didn't want to waste it, so he forced himself to ask, "Can cholera really kill a person in a few minutes? I didn't read that anywhere in there, but I heard a man say it at church."

"Did you read these magazines?" Dr. Drake asked.

"Yes. I. . .I want to be a doctor when I grow up," Henry blurted out.

"Well, well." Dr. Drake leaned against the porch rail. "I was a bit older than you when I read my cousin's medical books and decided the same thing. That's one of the great advantages of this country. Our citizens can choose what they want to be. Henry, if you set your mind to being a doctor, you can be one. Anyone can be anything he wants."

"He?" Rachel asked. "What about me?"

The doctor smiled. "I'm sure you'll make a wonderful wife and mother someday."

Rachel frowned but didn't respond.

"Henry, would you like to follow me on my rounds today to see what it's like to be a doctor?"

Henry gasped. Go with the important doctor? He couldn't imagine such an opportunity.

"I'll have to ask my mother. I'm helping with the cleanup at the Broadricks'."

"That's important. Why don't we do it next week, then? I'll talk to George about it and let you know a good day."

"Thank you, Dr. Drake," Henry said. "And thanks again for the magazines."

The doctor smiled and waved them on their way before he carried the magazines into the house.

Henry leaped off the porch.

"Rachel, can you believe that? I'm going to go with the doctor on his calls."

"Humph," she said. "I didn't know you wanted to be a doctor."

"I didn't either until a few days ago. It was just like it happened to Dr. Drake," he said with awe in his voice. "After I read the articles in his magazines, I thought that I'd like to help people get well. I'd like to stop cholera from killing people."

"He didn't tell you if people died in minutes or not," Rachel said.

Henry cocked his head in thought. "No, he didn't. I'll ask him again when I go with him next week. Oh, I hope we're not in school by then. But Father would let me go anyway since Dr. Drake is going to talk to him. This is too important."

"Well, it's not like you're going to be a doctor after you go with Dr. Drake for one day," Rachel said. "You could have asked my grandfather about cholera. He's a doctor."

"I haven't seen him since I learned about it," Henry said. "But now I get to go with Dr. Drake. He's a very important doctor."

"So is Grandpa Miller," Rachel said.

Henry nodded, and with one street to go until they reached the Broadricks', he yelled, "I'll race you!" He darted off to tell Mother the news. He looked back once. Rachel wasn't running. She was walking slowly back to the Broadrick sisters' home.

That afternoon they dipped more water out of the cellar. Henry had just changed jobs with Rachel, when she dipped a bucket, scooping the snake with the water. While the snake splashed around in the bucket, Henry ran in the house for a sack, and they poured the bucket of water, snake and all, into the sack. Water leaked right through, but the snake stayed in.

When Henry took over the dipping part again, he was relieved that he didn't have to watch for the snake. They were getting near the bottom of the cellar, and it was mighty dark inside. Rachel went for a lamp while Henry scooped up more water. Rotted apples and potatoes came with the last few scoops. He put his hands down to fill another bucket when something slithered over his fingers. He yelped, jumped back, and fairly flew up the cellar steps. Rachel was just coming out the back door with the lantern.

"Get the broomstick!" Henry yelled. "There's another snake down here."

He waited until she returned, and then he descended the

steps with the lantern turned up high. Rachel followed him, carrying the broom and the snake sack.

They followed the same procedure they had the week before and captured two more snakes before they thoroughly examined each cellar ledge and shelf. At last Henry breathed a sigh of relief that there were no more snakes in the house.

That night at dinner, discussion centered on Dr. Drake, who had been true to his word and talked to Father about Henry following him around one day next week.

"I didn't know you wanted to be a doctor," Father said at dinner.

"I do," Henry said. "I want to help people get well."

"A doctor in the family," Father said to Mother. "Our son, a doctor. What do you think of your brother, Louisa?"

"Dr. Lankford," Louisa said with a broad grin. "Would you pass the butter?"

CHAPTER 5

Following Dr. Drake

The most important day in Henry's life finally arrived. School wasn't in session yet, so Henry didn't have to worry about missing it. But Rachel was back for market day, and she had shown up on Henry's doorstep.

"Don't you need to help at the market?" Henry asked her when he answered the door.

"No. Mama said I could come over here."

"But I'm going over to Dr. Drake's house."

"Oh," Rachel said. She pressed her lips together and looked

at him as if she were waiting for something. A long silence stretched between them, and Rachel raised her eyebrows.

Henry knew what she wanted, but he wasn't going to say it. He didn't want her along. After all, Dr. Drake had invited him, not her.

"Good morning, Rachel," Mother called as she walked into the parlor. "Come on in. You're here bright and early."

Henry had no choice but to open the door and motion Rachel inside.

"Yes. I thought I'd be needed at market today, but Mama said I could come on over here."

"This is Henry's day to go with Dr. Drake."

"I already told her," Henry said. "And I'd better get going."

Rachel stood in front of the door and didn't move.

"Wait a minute," Mother said. "Rachel, did you want to go with him?"

"Mother," Henry said in protest.

"I'd be honored to go," Rachel said. "Thank you for asking." She turned and headed back out the door, and Henry followed.

"What if Dr. Drake says you can't come?" Henry asked.

"Why would he do that?"

Henry sighed. Dr. Drake was too much of a gentleman to insist that Rachel return home. He was stuck with her.

"Well, don't say anything. Just listen to him," he said as they approached Dr. Drake's home.

"I won't get in the way," Rachel said. "You won't even know I'm there."

"Why do you want to go on calls with him? You said you could ask your grandpa to take you."

"Maybe I want to see what's so great about Dr. Drake."

"Hummp." Henry led the way around Dr. Drake's house to the side entry of his office. He knocked and stood back as Dr. Drake opened the door.

"Henry, I've been looking forward to your visit," the doctor said. "Please come in."

Good manners dictated that Henry acknowledge Rachel. "Do you remember my cousin Rachel?"

Dr. Drake nodded. "Hello, Rachel. Why don't you look around? I'll be with you in a minute. I have a patient in my surgery."

He went into a separate room and shut the door behind him.

"What an odd place," Rachel said. "It doesn't look like Grandpa Miller's office. What are all these rocks?"

Henry had wondered the same thing. A glass-fronted display case held maybe fifty different rocks. One wall of the office was lined with bookcases, which held row after row of thick, leather-bound books. Henry walked over to the bookcase and examined them—medical books. So it was one of these that Dr. Drake had read when he was a little older than Henry and then decided to become a doctor.

In one corner of the room sat a large desk, and behind it stood a skeleton.

Rachel stared at it and moved over to touch its hand.

"Do you think this is real?" she asked.

"Of course, it's real. That's bone, isn't it? It sure isn't wood."

"I thought maybe it was animal bone, carved in these shapes, but it's not. This person was alive. This is creepy. Why wouldn't they have buried him? Or her? This could be a woman."

"It is a woman," Dr. Drake said from the doorway.

Rachel gasped, but Dr. Drake didn't elaborate. He ushered

his patient to the office door.

"That core will keep growing. The skin on the outside is dead. Only thing to do is cut it off from time to time, or you'll find yourself walking as if there were a stone in your boot. You can do it yourself with a sharp razor, but you must be careful not to go too deep."

The man thanked Dr. Drake and left.

"You said it's a woman," Rachel said, pointing at the skeleton. "Why is she here? Why didn't she get a proper burial? Mama says a person deserves a Christian burial."

"She was a. . .a derelict, an intemperate person."

Henry didn't understand, and from her furled brow, he didn't think Rachel did, either. For once he spoke up before she could. "What does that mean?"

Dr. Drake hesitated briefly, then answered, "She drank a lot of alcohol. She didn't have any relatives to claim her body when she died, so it was given to the medical school."

"That's horrible," Rachel said. Henry wished she had not come if she were going to insult the renowned doctor.

"It's not horrible, although I understand why you'd think so," Dr. Drake said, not seeming in the least insulted. "We can't learn about the human body's ills unless we know about the body. We need to see how the bones go together. We need to know how the organs function."

"But no proper burial?" Rachel repeated.

"The Bible says ashes to ashes," Dr. Drake said. "Her body would decompose anyway. It was her spirit she should have been concerned about. She made a contribution to society in death by having her body be used for science."

He walked over to the skeleton and patted its shoulder bone. "I don't know her real name, but I call her Betsy."

"Betsy! That's my mother's name," Rachel said.

Dr. Drake looked taken aback. "Well then, I'll have to change her name to Sarah." He turned to Henry. "This," he motioned toward the skeleton, "is part of observation in anatomy and physiology, and both studies are important in learning medicine. Next to God, a reliance on science and learning prepares you for the trials of life, and there are many in this profession. Do you think you are suited to be a doctor?"

"Oh, yes," Henry answered without hesitation. He wasn't about to admit that he found the skeleton as distasteful as Rachel. If Dr. Drake said it was important to study the human skeleton, then it was.

"Shall we go? I must call on Mrs. Ledbetter, who has a touch of the gout."

"What about these rocks?" Rachel asked as she walked past the glass case.

"I have some of them because of the minerals in them. Others contain fossils. The ones on the top shelf are from an Indian mound."

"You opened an Indian mound?" Rachel asked. "Isn't that like opening a grave?"

Dr. Drake considered the question for some time. "I suppose it is, although I didn't think of it that way when I excavated several mounds about fifteen years ago. Some of the mounds are thought to be a thousand years old, and I knew there could be a lot of history buried inside. Since farmers around here were plowing through the smaller ones, and even here in Cincinnati a street cut right through one, I felt the ones I excavated would have been destroyed anyway. The arrow points and beads over here," he motioned toward another shelf, "are from a mound."

"We have one on our farm," Rachel said, "but we leave it alone." She acted as if her way was the only way, and not for the first time, Henry wished she had not come with him.

"We won't need to go to the livery stable for my buggy," Dr. Drake said, changing the subject. "Mrs. Ledbetter lives only a few blocks away."

Henry walked beside Dr. Drake, while Rachel trailed behind. All the streets had not yet been cleared of the sludge from the flood, so it would have been hard to get a team and buggy through some sections of town.

"This must be cleaned up," Dr. Drake said, motioning to the flood debris. "When the cholera comes, it will be concentrated in filthy areas."

The cholera. Every time he heard that word, Henry's heart pounded faster. From the articles he'd read, it seemed to be an uncontrollable disease.

"How is it spread?" Henry asked. "Why will it be in the filthy areas?"

"I believe it's spread by poisonous, invisible flying insects. These insects breed in filthy areas, much like mosquitoes breed in marshy areas."

"Then one person can't give it to another person?" Henry asked. He glanced behind him and saw that Rachel was listening intently.

"No. It's not contagious. There's agreement among doctors about that. But there's disagreement on how it's spread. Still, I believe I'm right about the tiny insects carrying it and giving it to one person after another. I think the atmosphere has something to do with it, too. Reports from London say it's focused in the poorest areas, where there is neglect and filth. And those most vulnerable to the disease are the intemperate, like Bets—" He glanced at Rachel. "Like Sarah, my skeleton.

"Here we are," he said, stopping by a two-story house, not unlike the Broadrick sisters' home. "Mrs. Ledbetter doesn't know you're accompanying me today, so you'd better stay out here until I ask if she'll permit observation."

He went inside, leaving them on the porch. In front of the house, great mounds of sludge dried in the spring sunshine.

"They look like the Indian mounds," Rachel said. "Except they aren't as high. This place sure stinks."

"We haven't got the flood mounds in the Broadrick sisters' backyard dumped in the river," Henry thought out loud. "We have to do that before the cholera comes."

"Do you believe that part about tiny flying insects we can't see? That seems silly." Rachel plopped down in a clear spot on the porch step. "I don't think we get to go in."

A moment later, Dr. Drake came back outside. A deep frown had settled on his forehead. Rachel jumped up and stood beside Henry.

"We're going to see how Mr. Hamilton's leg is doing," Dr. Drake said.

"What about Mrs. Ledbetter?" Rachel asked.

"A fake practitioner has sold her some liniment. Probably snake oil!" he snorted. "The poor and uneducated can easily be sold strange medical notions, but I thought Mrs. Ledbetter was above that." He shook his head. "I constantly fight these quacks and imitators."

He set a brisk pace as he walked to his next patient's house. Henry was almost running beside the doctor, who took one step to every two of Henry's.

"Stay here," he said when they arrived at Mr. Hamilton's home. "I'll see if you'll be allowed inside."

Henry sat on the step with Rachel, but popped up a moment later when Dr. Drake reappeared. "You may come in," he said.

There wasn't much to see. Mr. Hamilton's broken leg was covered with splints, and Dr. Drake was more concerned with the fever that came and went than with the leg. He prescribed a medicine that Henry had never heard of, then the trio left and walked back toward Dr. Drake's home.

"When will people stop dumping their garbage in the streets?" Dr. Drake asked as they sidestepped pigs that were rooting in the decaying matter. "We have dead animals decomposing here with rotting vegetables. Is it any wonder that cholera will come?"

He continued giving a lecture about filth and the creeks and animal carcasses that had Rachel wide-eyed with wonder, and Henry figured he looked the same way. He'd seen Mill Creek in the fall and early winter when it ran bloody red from the pork slaughterhouses, but he hadn't thought about it as a problem, just as part of the seasonal cycle.

They were only a block from Dr. Drake's home when a young man charged toward them from the other direction.

"Dr. Drake. Thank God I've found you. We need you at the river. A man fell overboard."

"Is the Humane Society there?" Dr. Drake asked. Henry had never seen the Humane Society in action, although he'd heard of their daring rescues.

"Yes, they just pulled him out."

Dr. Drake broke into a run, and Henry and Rachel raced after him. A few moments later they reached the river. Several people surrounded a still form on the wharf. One man leaned over the drowning victim and pushed on his chest, then turned him on his side.

"Make way. Dr. Drake's here," the young man said in panting gasps.

Dr. Drake knelt beside the unconscious man and took over the resuscitating procedure. Not a full minute later, the man coughed and vomited river water. Dr. Drake continued working on the man until he coughed again and caught his breath.

"He's breathing," someone yelled, and a cheer went up from the crowd that had gathered.

If Henry had any doubts before that he wanted to be a doctor, he knew for sure now. He wanted to help people. He wanted to save lives. He wanted to be like Dr. Drake.

Fifteen minutes later, the man was walking around, as good as new.

"I'm awfully thirsty," he said, and the others laughed.

Dr. Drake, Henry, and Rachel once again started walking toward his house.

"He's a healthy specimen, and now that the Ohio is out of him, he seems fine," Dr. Drake said. "After I stop by home to see if anyone is waiting or there are any messages, I need to go over to the hospital to see some patients, and you won't be permitted to go in there."

At Dr. Drake's house, they went inside while he collected some old issues of medical magazines for Henry to read.

"When you return these, we'll talk again," Dr. Drake said.

They were almost to the door when Rachel turned back.

"Dr. Drake, is it true that a person can catch cholera and be dead in a few minutes?"

"No," he said emphatically. "Not in a few minutes. However, records show that death has come as soon as six hours after an attack."

CHAPTER 6

Independence Day

Henry read the magazines Dr. Drake had given him, but since they were old issues, there was no mention of cholera in them. They actually were issues of the magazine that Dr. Drake edited. The *Western Medical and Physical Journal* covered more than diseases and their causes and cures.

"How do you come up with all these writings?" Henry asked Dr. Drake when he returned the magazines for another pile.

"Studies," Dr. Drake replied. "I want to see how Western medicine differs from Eastern medicine, but I can't just give my ideas. I have to observe and then write down my conclusions."

"What kind of studies?" Henry asked. The way Dr. Drake

looked at him made him fear he had been too bold in asking.

"You're a curious boy, Henry, and that curiosity is going to take you far in life." In a low voice, as if musing aloud, he added, "You need direction, but you're too young for formal training." He walked over to his desk and sorted through a drawer, taking out a pencil and some paper.

"Henry, how would you like to help me with some scientific experiments?" he said as he drew some lines on the top sheet of paper.

"Oh, yes!"

Dr. Drake wrote some more, then looked up. "Here's what you do. Each day I want you to record the temperature of the air at your house, then down at the river. You'll need a thermometer. Do you have one?"

"No."

"I'll order one for you next time I need supplies."

"I've seen one in Luttman's Mercantile. Maybe Father would get it for me."

"I imagine he would. George has a curious mind, too, and he'd want to foster that in you. And what about your cousin?"

"Rachel?"

"She's got a questioning mind and an outspoken tongue," Dr. Drake said with a chuckle. "She wants something out of life, but she'll have to work hard to get it." Again this was said in such a low voice that Henry wondered if he was supposed to hear. It didn't matter; he didn't understand what Dr. Drake meant by it. What could Rachel want?

"Now, there are a few other studies you could do for me. One is to notice the clouds at two times each day and record the type. The times must be consistent—the same. And when you go to the river to measure the air temperature, you must leave the thermometer in the same place for a few minutes to get an accurate reading. Don't leave it in direct sunlight. While you're waiting, measure the depth of the river. Use the flood gauge at the public landing and record the direction of the wind, and the speed, too, if you can. Maybe Rachel would want to help you."

"She's only in town on market days, but I might let her help then."

With school starting up again after the flood cleanup, Henry made a schedule of when he could record his observations. That way they would be consistent. Father bought him a thermometer, which he kept in a leather pouch so it wouldn't break when he carried it to the river each morning before school. At that time he measured the river depth and looked up at the sky. After school, he again measured the river depth and recorded the type of clouds and where they were in the sky before he went to the shipyard to do his regular cleanup work. With the threat that cholera would come to Cincinnati, Father was a fanatic about keeping the place free of garbage.

"Why are you collecting all this information?" Rachel asked the first Saturday Henry took her with him on his scientific trip to the river.

"We're doing a study. We can see if the temperature affects any events that occur. Dr. Drake said cholera is affected by the atmosphere, but I'm not sure about the river. Maybe he wants to see if the temperature affects the height of the river."

At home on the porch, he showed her a book he had checked out of the library that had all types of clouds in it. "Those are storm clouds there," he said and pointed to the sky.

Rachel looked at him as if he were crazy. "Of course, they're storm clouds. Everybody knows that. It'll be raining in a few minutes. The breeze has cooled down, too."

Henry whipped his thermometer out of its leather pouch and set it against the porch rail. He sighed. Explaining this to Rachel was hard. She questioned everything he said.

"You know the saying: Red sky at night is a sailor's delight. Red sky at morning, sailor take warning."

"Sure. I know that. Cousin Richard says that all the time."

Her cousin Richard had been a sailor a long time ago during Mr. Madison's War, and he was always telling them stories about when he was kidnapped by the British.

"Well, Dr. Drake says we can prove that by scientific observations. If we record the looks of the sky in the morning and the sun shines pink and red on the clouds and later it rains, and that happens over and over in the same way, then we can draw a conclusion that when the sky looks like that, it will rain later in the day."

"We didn't have a red sky this morning," Rachel said.

"No, it doesn't mean we will always have a red sky before we get rain, but if there is a red sky, it will probably rain."

"We'll see. I might start some of my own observations."

"Dr. Drake would like that. He has doctors in other parts of the state making observations, too. He says next we'll record the different plant life so we see if it has any effect on things."

As spring moved toward summer, Henry continued to sweep up at the shipyard, but he also spent more time with his observations, and he added other items as well. He measured the distance around the big oak tree in his yard and other trees, too, but these he recorded weekly, not daily. He measured the height of the wild rose bush. He counted blossoms on one limb of the redbud tree and recorded the length of time that passed before the pink blooms fell off. Then he measured the tiny puckered leaves every day, and soon they were full-grown, flat, heart-shaped leaves.

"You are a natural scientist," Dr. Drake told him.

"Oh, but I want to be a doctor," Henry said.

"You will be someday, but first you must understand the world God gave us and what change brings what result. I'm proud of you."

Henry smiled, and he figured if he could measure his smile, it probably was the biggest one he had ever had.

Each week the temperatures on Henry's charts climbed. Then summer arrived, and plans were made for the big Fourth of July celebration.

"After the parade and speeches," Mother said a couple days before the event, "everyone will come here. George, you're to fetch the Broadrick sisters. Betsy's family will be here early, so Henry and Rachel can set up the big table in the yard before the parade. Then we'll use all the quilts to sit on. George, can you bring some lumber from the shipyard so we can put together some benches?"

"I'll take care of it," Father assured her.

The evening of the third, Father drove home a wagon filled with plenty of boards for benches. Henry helped him unload the lumber and foot-and-a-half lengths of wide tree trunks, which Father had cut for bases. With well-placed nails, Father made sturdy benches for their guests.

"It's right that we celebrate this holiday with family and

friends in this great nation," Father said when they stood back and surveyed their work.

"Are you going to give a speech?" Henry asked.

Father looked surprised. "A speech? No."

"You sound like a speechmaker." Henry waved an arm out as if gesturing to a crowd. "In this great nation," he mimicked his father's deep voice.

Father chuckled. "I guess I sound like a politician when I'm just a proud American. This country gives us freedom—freedom to speak what we feel; freedom to worship as we believe; freedom to become anything we want."

"Dr. Drake said that, too. I can be anything I want to be as long as I set my mind to it."

"He meant you can be anything as long as you're willing to work for it. And you're a good worker, Henry." Father ruffled Henry's hair. "Let's go in and see if your mother's got supper ready."

It was hard to sleep that night. Besides being hot and stuffy in his loft bedroom, Henry's expectations of the next day kept him awake.

The Fourth of July dawned with no red skies. It would be a good day, Henry thought as he downed his oatmeal in big gulps. Rachel's family arrived early, and Rachel raced to the river with him to make his morning recordings.

When they returned, they helped carry the big table to the yard. Aunt Betsy set her pies on one corner and covered them with a cloth to keep the flies out.

"This is to keep you out, too," she told Henry with a laugh.

By late morning, they stood on the side of the street, watching the Independence Day parade. Hundreds marched by them, waving. Some men represented trade associations. Children marched with their Sunday schools. A festive air surrounded them all as the nation's freedoms were celebrated.

"Do you want to listen to the speeches?" Rachel asked.

"Maybe one," Henry said, "if it doesn't go too long."

"Politicians always speak too long," Rachel said, but she walked with Henry to the end of the parade route, where the speaker's stand had been erected. The first speaker had the crowd's attention, and roars of approval filled the air as he punctuated every accolade for the United States of America with his fist in the air. But after an hour, Henry was tired of standing, tired of listening, and was hot and hungry.

"Want to go home now?" he whispered to Rachel, so he wouldn't upset those around him who were listening to the orator.

She nodded.

They edged their way out of the crowd, then headed toward home. Under the shade trees in the backyard, they found the Broadrick sisters visiting with Mother and Aunt Betsy. On a pallet lay Rachel's three-year-old sister, Alice, sound asleep. Her little brother, Calvin, played with Henry's dog, Jackson.

"Are the speeches over?" Mother asked.

"No. I think they'll go on for a while," Henry said. He drew some cool water from the well, and he handed the dipper to Rachel. She drank a dipperful, then Henry drank one. "Listening to how great this country is sure makes a person thirsty."

"It was probably the hot sun and not the words," Rachel said.

Over two hours later the others arrived in separate

groups. First Henry's grandparents arrived, then Rachel's grandparents; her cousin Richard Allerton and his wife and Timothy and Pamela; and Ben Allerton and his wife and new baby daughter; plus Father and Uncle Andrew. The backyard was filled with laughter and talk until the women uncovered the food.

"Let us thank God for the providence He's given us," Father said. The others stood and bowed their heads.

"Thank you, our heavenly Father, for the joys of this day. We live in the greatest country in the world because we are free. And the greatest freedom we have is to worship You in any manner we choose. Please guide us to make choices that will please You. And bless this food to our bodies that we may be stronger and serve You better. In Jesus' name, Amen."

"Amen" echoed through the gathering.

The adults filled their plates from the large table. Then it was the children's turn to heap fried chicken, cornbread, green beans, and boiled potatoes onto their plates. After they'd eaten all the pies, someone called out for some music, and Aunt Betsy retrieved her violin from the Farley wagon.

"Did you bring your violin?" she asked Richard. "Although, by rights, this should be yours."

Henry had heard the story before of how Richard had taught Aunt Betsy to play his violin, then had entrusted the instrument to her when he went to sea. He had no idea he would be kidnapped by the British and have to serve a foreign master until his escape several years later. He had returned to Boston, then come west to Cincinnati to start a new life. Aunt Betsy had offered his violin to him then, but he had refused to take it. Instead he had bought a new one and let her keep the one she had treasured.

Richard was already walking toward the back door. "I put it in the house," he said and disappeared inside. A moment later he came out carrying his violin.

They tuned up, and Richard called out, "What's your favorite?"

Miss Emma named a tune, and the two violinists jumped into the song. Others sang along and called out more favorites. After awhile Father lit lanterns and placed them among the group.

It was well after dark when Richard and Betsy put their violins away and the group broke up. Henry helped carry empty baskets to the wagons lined up in front of his house. Father escorted the Broadrick sisters to a wagon and left to take them home. The others bid farewell into the night. Rachel's family was the last to leave.

"Thanks for the hospitality," Aunt Betsy called to Mother.

"Another great Independence Day," Henry said to Rachel. "The best country in the world—where we have freedom. We can all be anything we want to be as long as we set our minds to it."

"Not all of us," Rachel said as she climbed onto the wagon.

Now what did she mean by that? Henry wondered.

CHAPTER 7

News from New York

With the big Fourth of July celebration over, Henry settled down to helping his dad at the shipyard a few hours every day, but he still had time to record his observations and occasionally visit with Dr. Drake.

Every time Rachel came to town, she somehow slipped away from the market stall to find Henry. Even if he was at the shipyard, she came by.

"Have you seen Dr. Drake this week?" she asked one hot mid-July day. "I thought I'd see if I could borrow a book from him."

"A book on what?" Henry asked as he put his broom away. He'd finished his chores for the day, so he might as well see what Rachel had on her mind.

"I want to know more about the bones in his skeleton."

Together they walked toward Dr. Drake's, but they met him on the street a block from his home.

"It's here," Dr. Drake said in a solemn voice. "The cholera is in New York."

Henry gasped. Now the dreaded disease wasn't just something spreading in Europe that he read about in magazines. Now it was in the United States. How long until it reached Cincinnati?

"When will it get here?" Rachel asked the question before Henry could speak.

"Hard to say. Could be a few weeks, could be a few months. We must get people to clean up the filth here. We must get rid of the breeding places for cholera."

"How did it get here?" Henry asked.

"Must have come on a ship. The report I have from a doctor friend in the East is rather sketchy." He held up a letter. "The disease reached New York nearly a month ago."

"A month?"

"Yes. There's no time to lose. I'm on my way to talk to some of the Board of Health members. The city must take precautions. We must insure the safety of our citizens." He raised a hand in farewell and marched on down the street.

Henry and Rachel stood looking at each other.

"It's here," Henry said, echoing Dr. Drake's words. "We must warn the others."

With wings on his feet, he ran back to the shipyard. Rachel kept pace with him.

The moment he saw his father, he yelled, "The cholera's in New York."

Father dropped the hammer he was holding and rushed to Henry's side.

"Who told you?"

"Dr. Drake. He thinks it came on a boat."

"Then it will probably come here the same way," Father said. He looked toward the Ohio River. "Every boat should be inspected before it's allowed to tie up at the wharf. If there's sickness on it, it can't stop here. I'll go talk to Dr. Drake."

"He's not home. He's talking to some Board of Health members."

"I'll find him. Go tell Mother."

Henry and Rachel raced home. As soon as they broke the news to Mother, they headed for the marketplace to tell Aunt Betsy. The news spread like wildfire through the market.

At the dinner table that night, Henry wasn't surprised at the sentiment in Father's grace.

"Our heavenly Father, thank You for this day and this food. Please deliver us from the pestilence of cholera that's in New York. . . ."

Henry didn't listen to the rest, but he added his own fervent prayer to that of his father's. *Please, God, don't let cholera kill my family.*

"Dr. Drake has called a meeting of all interested citizens tonight," Father said. "I'm going to hear what he has to say."

"Can I go with you?" Henry asked.

Father looked at Mother, then shook his head. "You'd better stay here. I'll tell you what he says when I get home. Or maybe tomorrow. It may be late when I get back."

Henry went to bed in the loft and watched the stars out his window. He could hear the mantle clock ticktock, ticktock, and still Father didn't return. What could they be discussing this long? He fell asleep dreaming that the invisible cholera insects hovered over Cincinnati.

At first light, Henry was awake and rushed downstairs. He smelled coffee and found Mother and Father in the kitchen.

"What did he say?" Henry demanded.

"The afternoon newspaper will have a full report," Father said, "if I miss telling you anything. Mostly what Dr. Drake said was that we must clean up the marshy areas where the disease can breed. We must clean out cellars and air them. Garbage must be disposed of properly so it won't make our drinking water impure. It's up to the citizens to clean up this town. The Board of Health doesn't have any money to hire people, so we have to do it ourselves. There are places where the flood sludge hasn't been properly disposed of. These are the breeding places."

Henry's mouth formed a large O. "We didn't get the big pile out of the Broadricks' backyard," he said.

Father sat up straight. "You're right, Henry. How did we forget that? This evening I'll bring a wagon over and we'll clean that out. What about their cellar? Did you get it good and dry? Go look at it before you come to the shipyard today."

"I'll air out our cellar," Mother said. "Louisa can help me carry things out."

Henry called on the Broadrick sisters and told them of the coming disease and the plan to remove the dried sludge pile in the backyard that evening.

"I didn't want to say anything about it," Miss Emma said. "But I did wonder about it."

"We'll take care of it. And the cellar," Henry said.

He didn't want to go down into the cellar, just in case he

and Rachel had missed a snake when they were draining the place. So it was with much trepidation that he opened the outside door, which let in quite a bit of light. Still, he carried a lantern when he descended the steps into the gloominess. A musty smell combined with a rancid odor. The dirt floor was still muddy, and low places held water.

He looked around, but caught no movement that would signal that something other than spiders lurked in the corners.

He climbed the steps to the kitchen entrance.

"It's still wet," he said as he set the lantern on the table.

"We'll keep the outside door open during daylight hours," Miss Hannah said. "A few days ought to dry it out. When does Dr. Drake say the cholera will come?"

"He doesn't know. He just says it will come."

On Sunday the minister commented on the flurry in Cincinnati as townspeople cleaned up the garbage in the streets and aired out cellars.

"But it isn't enough for you good people to take care of your own. You must reach out to those less fortunate and help them. Down by the river is an area of filth that must be taken care of."

That was not an area that Henry took much note of. Oh, he passed nearby when he went to the river to measure the depth, but Mother had warned him to stay away from the squalor and degradation of that area.

Now that it had been brought to his attention, he decided to investigate on his Sunday afternoon trip to measure the river. First he talked to his friend Raleigh in the churchyard and convinced him to go along. Later that afternoon the two boys walked purposefully to the edge of what could only be described as a shantytown. Men sat outside small, clustered shacks and drank liquor. Women cuddled up beside them. Dead animals rotted in the gutters. Garbage stank in the hot sun.

"My mother would skin me alive if she knew I was down here," Henry said. "I just wanted to see what the preacher was talking about. This is sure a place where the invisible cholera insects could breed. Dr. Drake thinks there's something in the air that makes them come to places like this."

"It's the stink," Raleigh said. "Let's get out of here."

Henry quickly marked down his observations and the boys hurried home.

A few days later, Rachel was back in town on market day. She was to deliver some fresh eggs to the Broadrick sisters, but she had walked by Henry's house early that morning and now accompanied him to measure the river. He confided in her about his trip to see the squalid area.

"Show me," she said.

"It wouldn't be fitting for you to see it," Henry said.

"Why not? You saw it, and I'm older than you."

"You're a girl. Girls aren't supposed—"

"I'm tired of hearing what girls aren't supposed to do," Rachel said. "I'm going down there. You coming?" She turned and marched toward the shantytown. Henry raced after her.

"There's probably nobody there," he said when he caught up with her. "I was here on Sunday. They'd be working today."

But they weren't working. Even that early in the morning, groups of men, with a few women here and there, sat around on crates. The stench was as great as it had been on Sunday—maybe worse, as more fly-covered garbage had been added to the stinking piles around the shacks.

"Why are they here?" Rachel asked.

"Maybe they don't have jobs," Henry said.

"They could come to the country and farm. There's land enough for everybody. Don't they know that?"

"Hey, what you got there?" a rough-looking man hollered at them. He approached them with a stagger to his walk.

All Henry held was his pencil and the paper he made his daily observations on, and he quickly stuffed them in his pocket. Surely the man couldn't mean them. He glanced at Rachel. He'd forgotten she carried eggs that she was going to deliver to the Broadrick sisters. She stuck the small basket behind her back.

"Gimme those, girlie," the ruffian demanded and grabbed Rachel's arm.

She screamed and dropped the basket. Henry jumped on the man, but the burly fellow shook him off. With the basket in his grip, the man turned around, and Rachel yelled, "Run."

Henry didn't need a second warning. He was on Rachel's heels, but he could still hear the awful man's boisterous laughter follow them.

They didn't stop running until they were two streets away from the shantytown.

"Are you all right?" Henry asked when he could catch his breath.

"Yes, but Mama's going to be mad about that basket. And what will I tell Miss Emma about her eggs?" She shook her head, then she added. "That thief got a bunch of broken eggs. I dropped that basket hard."

"You shouldn't have gone over there," Henry said.

"You shouldn't have told me about it."

"I didn't say you should go."

The argument would have continued because Henry was just warming up, but when they turned down another street, they saw a commotion a couple blocks away. A crowd was gathering.

"Smoke," he yelled, as soon as he saw spirals of black curling toward the sky.

"The hotel," Rachel shouted as they raced down the street.

Men and women alike poured out of nearby buildings. Many carried buckets, and one man yelled above the roar of the crowd, "Form a line. Start a brigade."

Henry and Rachel joined the ranks of townspeople who stretched in a line to the river. A couple men filled buckets and handed them to the first in line. Henry had to carry the bucket twenty feet to Rachel, but soon others filled in the gaps and the sloshing buckets changed hands quickly.

Another line had formed to the closest brick cistern, but it soon ran out of water, and the line shifted to another cistern.

The fire was raging, and even from his place in line, Henry could see flames on the roof and hear glass windows shattering from the heat.

Henry's boots were wet. His trousers were wet. But the cold river water that spilled on him felt good in the early August heat. He glanced at Rachel, who was working as hard as he was, passing the full buckets toward the hotel and passing the empty buckets back toward the river.

Down the line he saw Richard Allerton, who had played his violin at the Independence Day picnic. Father and the men from the shipyard were near him. The entire town had turned out to help put out the fire, but they didn't seem to be making any headway.

At least the wind wasn't blowing. There was hardly a breeze. It hadn't even moved Henry's wind scale that morning when he'd recorded the reading.

Within two hours, the hotel had burned to the ground. Thanks to the townspeople's tenacity, the buildings around it hadn't caught on fire. They had doused them with water once they saw there was no hope of saving the hotel.

The lines disbanded and groups milled around, even though the charred remains of the building continued to smolder and send thin wisps of smoke heavenward.

Henry and Rachel hurried to join Father and Richard, who stood in a group with a couple other men.

"We've got to do something about it," Richard was saying. "We could patrol the areas at night, since most of the fires occur then. It's odd someone could start this one without being seen, but from the way it went up, it had to have been set."

"Someone set the fire?" Henry asked.

"It appears that way," Father said. "It started at two different ends of the hotel. That's mighty suspicious. Hard to believe that two accidental fires could start at about the same time in the same hotel."

"The sawmill went up the same way," Richard said.

"And that steamship," another man added.

"There's definitely an arsonist on the loose," Father said. "And now there's one more area to clean up before the cholera comes."

CHAPTER 8
Cholera!

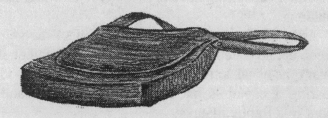

More fires were set through August, even though Henry's father joined the volunteer group that patrolled the downtown area at night. Henry watched the elegant Pearl Street House burn to the ground, but he heard rumors that it would be rebuilt. Two more steamboats burned, and then it seemed the arsonist had done all the damage he wanted. By September the volunteer arsonist control group disbanded, without ever catching the arsonist, and Father was home again at night.

Life settled into a new routine as school started the fall session. Mother had sprinkled chloride of lime in the yard and in the cellar and in the outhouse as part of her cleanup and as a possible deterrent to the cholera. Henry got the white powder on his shoes when he walked to school, and he left footprints wherever he went.

Of course, the stuff was spread in other places, too, because many townspeople thought it would keep them safe from cholera. Henry saw a few areas where it was dumped on top of garbage instead of the garbage being taken to the middle of the river.

Henry continued his practice of going to the river twice a day to measure the depth and record the air temperature, the cloud formations, and the wind direction. The skies had never been brighter nor the air as clean as on a late September afternoon after school, when Henry stood on the wharf making his notations.

Although he knew he should go on to the shipyard to sweep up, he watched a steamship approach and dock. There wasn't the usual activity aboard. Something was odd. A man wearing a captain's hat scurried off the boat and looked about in a frantic manner.

"Hey, boy!" he called out.

"Me?" Henry answered, pointing a thumb at his chest.

The captain strolled quickly to his side and said in a quiet voice, "We need a doctor. Can you fetch one?"

Henry gasped. "Cholera?" he asked.

The captain ignored his question. "Can you get a doctor?"

"Yes. I'll be right back," Henry said and ran as fast as he could to Vine Street. "Dr. Drake, Dr. Drake!" he yelled the entire block before he reached the house.

Dr. Drake met him on the porch.

"Henry, what's the matter? You could raise the dead with that kind of shouting."

Henry glanced first one direction, then the other. "I think cholera is here," he whispered. "A steamboat captain has asked for a doctor."

Dr. Drake turned white, then laid his hand over his heart. "God help us through the soul-trying days ahead. Take me to him. Then I want you to run as fast as you can away from there."

"But you said we couldn't catch it from other people."

"That's true. But we don't know where the invisible insects may be."

When Henry and the doctor got to the river, no one from the ship was on land. But as soon as they clomped onto the wooden wharf, the captain appeared on deck and disembarked.

"I'm Dr. Daniel Drake. What is it? Cholera?" he asked without waiting for the captain to identify himself.

"We need to bury three, and two more are ill."

"We are as ready as we'll ever be," Dr. Drake said resignedly. "I have a pesthouse set up, and the red flag is ready. I'll get a wagon."

The captain returned to the ship, and Dr. Drake looked off in the distance, then down at Henry.

"Go. Go quickly. Now! Go!" With each word his voice grew stronger, and Henry turned and ran.

When he was a block away, he hid behind the corner of a building and waited for Dr. Drake to return with a wagon. A few minutes later, Henry saw the victims being taken ashore and placed in the wagon. It rumbled off in the opposite direction of Henry's hiding place. He didn't know where the quarantine house was, but he'd heard talk that no one wanted it near them, so he suspected it was on the edge of town.

Father would know. Faster than he'd ever run, Henry raced to the shipyard. He didn't stop until he stood directly in front of Father. He didn't yell the news. He whispered it in a voice that was filled with the fear that had seized his heart.

"Dr. Drake just took two people from a steamboat to the pesthouse. Three more are dead."

"Cholera?" Father asked in a quiet voice.

Henry nodded.

"Go tell your mother, and stay at home the rest of today."

"But what about the sweeping up?"

"Go on home. Go!" Henry heard the same urgency in Father's voice that had been in Dr. Drake's.

He started walking home, but had only gone a few yards when he quickened his step, and then he was running. Heaving breaths burned his lungs before he got home. He rushed inside and slammed the door behind him.

Louisa poked her head from the kitchen doorway. "What's wrong? You look like you've seen a ghost."

"I've seen cholera," Henry said.

"Cholera?" Louisa seemed to choke on the word. "Mother?"

"Where is it?" Mother demanded in a low voice as she walked toward Henry.

"Brought in on a ship, just like Dr. Drake predicted. He's taking two people to the pesthouse."

Mother sat down hard on a chair in the parlor. "We need to warn the others. Did you tell Father?"

"Yes, he sent me home and said to stay here."

"All right. Get the lime and spread it in the yard and on the street in front of here. I'm going to tell the Broadrick sisters and warn the preacher."

Once Mother left, Henry got the bag of chloride of lime and sprinkled it outside. Would it kill the invisible cholera insects? Or would it keep the vapors that attracted the insects from forming? Dr. Drake had mentioned that atmospheric conditions affected the spread of cholera. But it was a beautiful Indian summer day outside. How could there be any disease in this clear air?

"I'm scared, Henry," Louisa said when he returned inside. "What do we do? Can we go to school tomorrow?"

"I don't know," he said.

At supper, Father prayed for the safety of Cincinnati, then shared his news from the quarantined house.

"Dr. Drake has treated everyone onboard the steamship with calomel, and the ship has anchored near the Kentucky side of the river. The dead have already been buried and all their belongings burned."

"What's calomel?" Louisa asked.

"A laxative. It makes you go to the bathroom," Father explained, and Louisa blushed.

"This may be insensitive, Louisa," Mother said, "but you should know about the disease."

"Dr. Drake told me it's like poisoning," Henry said. "A person's insides hurt something fierce."

"Can we go to school tomorrow?" Louisa asked.

Father and Mother exchanged a glance, then Mother said, "We are not going to panic about this. Perhaps Dr. Drake can isolate the cases, and it won't spread. You can go to school, and we'll wait and see what happens."

"It's not contagious," Henry said. "It can't be spread from one person to the next. Dr. Drake is certain of that."

"It seems awfully strange to me," Mother said. "I don't understand how invisible insects can cause it. Wouldn't the insects be carried by one person to the next? Isn't that what contagious means? Like smallpox?"

Henry wasn't sure himself, but he had heard Dr. Drake speak to this question many times, and he quoted his hero.

"Once you get smallpox, you can't get it again. But you can catch cholera over and over."

"Then why have the pesthouse?" Mother asked.

Father answered that one. "It's so the townspeople won't panic. So that they feel there is something being done. Dr. Drake had a hard time finding a building, and the one he got is rundown. But it will serve the purpose."

"I don't understand," Louisa said, "but I pray none of us will get it."

On Saturday, when Rachel came to market day, she said the same thing, and on Sunday the preacher led the congregation in prayer and then preached about cholera as a divine imposition.

"This plague is a punishment from God's own hand," he boomed. "It is a scourge to the thoughtless and immoral among us. Those who have weakened themselves by intemperance and living in filth have called this punishment on themselves.

"There have been four deaths in the squalor down by the river," he announced, and the congregation gave a collective gasp.

Henry sat up straighter. This was news to him. He needed to talk to Dr. Drake. After he recorded his daily observations, he would walk over to the doctor's house.

"We will observe our own day for prayer and fasting since President Jackson will not declare one for the nation," the preacher continued. "On Wednesday our congregation will lead the way by fasting and praying to avert the cholera."

Over Sunday dinner, with just their four family members, Louisa asked why the president wouldn't help the nation get over cholera.

"That's not exactly what the preacher meant," Father said. "President Jackson wouldn't declare a day of prayer because he thought that decision should be left to churches. Our country was founded on religious freedom, and I believe the president was right in keeping government and churches separate. We don't want one church's beliefs forced on us. We won't tell other churches when to have a day of prayer, and they sure can't tell us."

Discussion followed about cholera and what could be done about it. After his second piece of Mother's blackberry cobbler, Henry pushed his chair back and said he was going to record his observations.

"You don't need to go to the river," Mother said. "I thought Dr. Drake wanted your observation reports as something to do with the cholera coming. Well, it's come." She sounded angry, as if the reports were supposed to stop the cholera, and they hadn't.

"Father?" Henry appealed to his other parent. "I won't go near the shantytown. I promise."

Father looked at Mother. "I don't think you need to measure the river today. However, I'll go with you if you want to talk to Dr. Drake."

How had Father known what he wanted to do? Henry's wonder must have shown on his face because Father said with a grin, "I want to talk to him myself."

They called on Dr. Drake at midafternoon, but he wasn't there.

"He must be at the pesthouse," Father said. "Let's go see if Miss Hannah's feeling better. Then we'll see if Dr. Drake's home."

The Broadrick sisters had not gone to church with them

that morning. Miss Hannah had fallen a couple of days earlier and was feeling poorly. Miss Emma had told Father that morning when he had gone to fetch them to church. She hadn't wanted to leave her sister alone.

"Hannah's resting in bed," Miss Emma said once they were seated in the parlor. "She's not doing very well."

Henry glanced around the room. Pictures hung on newly whitewashed walls, and the furniture shined with polish. Who would have guessed that six months ago, this room had been underwater?

"Is there anything she needs that we could bring her?" Father asked.

"She's partial to apples," Miss Emma said.

"Rachel may bring some early apples in on market day," Henry said. "She did yesterday. I'll see what she has next time."

"That would be real nice of you, Henry," Miss Emma said.

They visited a few more minutes, and then Father and Henry walked back over to Vine Street.

Dr. Drake still wasn't there, but they sat on the porch and waited, and within a few minutes, Henry saw the doctor's horse and buggy down the street. Father pushed himself off the porch step and walked out to the street. Henry followed.

"We heard there were four deaths by cholera in the shantytown," Father said before Dr. Drake could even climb down off the high seat.

"That was by yesterday evening. There are eight more today."

"Eight more?" Henry asked. "Eight?"

"And I have seven severe cases in the pesthouse. I'm

going back there in a few minutes."

"It's spreading fast," Father said as they walked to the porch.

"Yes. The invisible cholera insect is breeding at an alarming rate. I can almost see them hovering above that filthy area." Dr. Drake leaned against a column on the front porch. His features were drawn, and he looked as if he hadn't slept in days.

"You can see them?" Henry asked.

Dr. Drake closed his eyes a moment before he answered. "No. In my mind I can see them, and when my eyes are open, I can imagine them as a vapor rising from the filth and garbage. I'm afraid they won't long be content to remain in that area."

Father cleared his throat. "I know that you said this isn't contagious, but it's hard to convince people of that. Patricia is fearful. She's covered our yard with lime, and she doesn't want Henry and Louisa to go back to school."

Henry stared at Father. He hadn't known Mother was thinking of keeping him away from school.

"Fear is a powerful emotion," Dr. Drake said. "It could predispose a body to be attacked by a malady."

A frown formed on Father's forehead. "Are you saying that if a person is fearful, she has a greater chance of getting cholera?"

"Any violent emotion could weaken a body's constitution," Dr. Drake said. "And fear is one of the strongest emotions."

"She wouldn't let me go to the river to make my observations," Henry said. "She's awfully afraid of this."

"I imagine she's afraid not for herself, but for her family," Dr. Drake said.

"But the fear, whether for herself or for Henry and Louisa, is still the same debilitating emotion. Is that right?" Father asked.

Dr. Drake nodded. "What are you thinking, George?"

"I'm going to send my family away from Cincinnati. To the country," he said. "Henry, how would you like to spend a few weeks on the farm with Rachel?"

CHAPTER 9

Country Life

On Monday morning, Henry, Louisa, and Mother packed their clothing and some bedding, and Father loaded up the wagon.

Henry's friend Raleigh was walking to school when the Lankford family passed him on their way out of town.

"Tell Mr. Harrington that we've gone to the country," Henry called. "We're going to stay with Rachel for a while."

Raleigh's mouth dropped open in amazement. Henry understood. He felt the same way about the fact that he was on his way to Rachel's instead of heading to school.

"When will you be back?" Raleigh yelled over the clomping of the horses' hooves and the squeaks and clanking of the big wagon wheels turning.

Henry glanced at Mother, then he shouted back, "When the cholera's gone."

The seven-mile journey to Rachel's house took about an hour and a half, but it seemed longer. Henry gained a new respect for Rachel's early rising, because she was in town on market days not long after sunup. She had to leave the farm in the dark.

Henry hadn't been to the farm in a long time. Since Rachel's family came to town at least twice a week for market, there didn't seem to be a need to make the journey to the country to see his distant cousin.

"Do they know we're coming?" Henry asked Mother.

"Not yet. But they won't mind, I'm sure. Betsy mentioned the other day that it might be safer in the country."

Yes, Rachel had said the same thing the last time he'd seen her. "How can you stand it in town with cholera around, and thieves, and fires and floods, and filth and pigs everywhere, and the smell?"

She had gone on and on about the glories of country life, but Henry noticed she'd sure made it to town for the Independence Day parade. She'd visited when the circus came to town last year, and she'd looked at the books that Mother had checked out of the library for him. She'd found one about bones because she hadn't borrowed one from Dr. Drake, but Henry had no idea why that seemed so important to her.

Father guided the horses around the last long curve. Rachel's house sat at the end of the lane with a big barn behind it. To the side stood the smokehouse, and other outbuildings were scattered here and there.

Aunt Betsy must have heard their arrival, for she came out on the front porch of the two-story farmhouse before Father stopped the team. Little Alice stood beside her and held onto her long skirt.

"Well, what brings you folks out here?" Aunt Betsy asked with a big smile.

"The cholera's gaining strength," Father said. "I'd be much obliged if my family could stay here awhile."

"You know you're welcome here anytime for as long as you like," Aunt Betsy said. She reached for a valise. "What's happening in town?"

"People are dying right and left," Mother said as she climbed off the wagon. "Henry, take this bag." She turned back to Aunt Betsy. "I couldn't rest easy with the children in school and cholera lurking who knows where."

"The fresh air out here is just what you need," Aunt Betsy said. "I'll put you and George in the front bedroom."

"I'm not staying," Father said. "But I'll be back on Sunday when the shipyard's closed."

"George, is it safe?" Aunt Betsy asked.

"I'll be fine. My men need their pay for their families, so we have to keep the shipyard open. We've spread lime all around the yard, so we'll be fine," he reassured her again and smiled at Mother.

"Where's Rachel?" Henry asked.

"She and Calvin are at school. Come on. Let's get you settled. Then we'll at least have something to eat before you go, George. Or can you stay until tomorrow?"

"No, I've got to get back," he answered.

They carried their belongings inside and gave the horses water. Then Aunt Betsy fixed the noon meal. As soon as

Uncle Andrew came in from the far pasture and they ate, Father hitched the horses to the wagon and headed back to town.

Mother stayed on the front porch until he was around the big curve and out of sight. Henry saw her wipe away a tear before she took a deep breath and smiled a tight smile.

"Father will be okay, won't he?" Henry asked.

"He'll be fine. He said he would, and he will," she said. "And every minute he's away, I will implore God to help George keep his word." She took another deep breath and turned toward the front door. "Let's see if we can be of help to Betsy."

But there wasn't much for Henry to do. "Rachel did the morning chores before she went to school. You can help her tomorrow morning," Aunt Betsy told Henry. "If you'd like, you can walk down by the creek. Maybe take measurements like you did in town."

That sounded like a good idea, so Henry took his pencil and paper that he had carefully packed and walked down to the creek. Louisa tagged along for something to do.

"Do you think we'll go to school with them tomorrow?" she asked.

"I don't know. I reckon we might. Be better than sitting around," Henry said.

They walked through a field where dead cornstalks crackled in the breeze, then through a brushy area, and finally to the creek. It wasn't a river, and it couldn't compare to the mighty Ohio, but Henry liked the gurgling sound the water made as it rushed around an area of built-up rocks, the place where Rachel crossed the creek.

Henry needed a good place to do a measurement, and it

had to be the same place each time. He picked up a long stick and gingerly stepped near a steep bank where the water flowed by only a foot from the top. There was no flood pole to use as a measure, so he stuck the stick in the water. It was deep here, at least deeper than the three-foot stick he'd found. He laid down on the bank and wagged the stick around, thrusting his hand into the cold water, but the stick didn't touch bottom.

"I need a longer stick. Maybe a pole," he said. The water was deceptively clear and deep. He looked around under nearby trees, but he couldn't find a stick that was strong enough and long enough for his measuring stick.

"Rachel can find one when she comes home," Louisa said.

But when Rachel got home, she told him she already had a measuring place, and they didn't need another one. With her pet crow on her shoulder, she showed him the huge chestnut tree downstream whose trunk was submerged in the water.

"The creek's eaten away the bank on this side, so I measure how high or low it is from this notch on the bark," she said and showed him. "This is the normal height. Right here."

"Right here," the crow mimicked.

Henry couldn't argue with her method, even though he wanted to.

"Your bird talks?" he asked, changing the subject.

"He fell out of a nest as a baby, and I fed him worms and milk until he was stronger," she said proudly. "Echo repeats what I say."

There was something about Rachel's attitude that bothered Henry. She thought the country was so much better than the city, and she didn't mind telling him so time and time again.

"The cholera won't come out here," she boasted. "We don't have the filth you have in town."

She was right again, but Henry didn't want to be reminded of that. He didn't want to think about his father and Dr. Drake being in the city with the invisible cholera insects. He wished they could be seen. Then people could swat them, smash them, and kill them so they wouldn't harm anyone. But how could they fight something that was invisible?

"You might as well go to school with Rachel and Calvin," Mother said that evening. "We don't know how long we'll be here, so you can continue in your reader and surprise Mr. Harrington with your progress when we go back home. And you can help Rachel with early chores by gathering eggs."

Henry went to bed that night on a pallet on the floor of the front bedroom. Mother and Louisa shared the bed. He listened to Mother's goodnight prayer and whispered one of his own for the safety of his father and his friends in Cincinnati.

Before daylight the next morning, Henry felt a nudge on his shoulder. A moment later the nudge was a shake, and he opened his eyes to darkness.

"Time to get up, sleepyhead," Rachel said. "You're supposed to help with the eggs this morning. Father will take them to market tomorrow."

Henry nodded and dressed quickly. In the kitchen he took the basket that Aunt Betsy handed him.

"We appreciate your help, Henry," she said as she put a piece of wood in the cookstove. "Rachel's already in the barn milking. I'll have breakfast ready when you finish chores."

Henry walked to the henhouse, holding a lantern in front

of him. During the day, the hens ran loose in the yard, but at night they were closed in to roost. The door squeaked as he opened it, and the hens clucked at the disturbance.

Aunt Betsy had said he should shoo the hens off the nests and collect the eggs. It couldn't be that hard, could it? He set the lantern down in the center of the henhouse and started with the first nest on the side opposite the door.

The first three went fine. The hens made a racket, but they ambled off the nests and he collected several eggs.

The fourth hen must have awakened on the wrong side of the nest. She wouldn't move when he poked at her. Instead, she pecked him! He jerked his hand back with a yelp. He tried it again, and she pecked him again, harder this time. She'd drawn blood.

Henry moved on down the room. He'd come back to that one. He successfully ousted all the other hens except the reddish-colored one that had pecked him. A few hens milled around the room, and others returned to their nests. He tried to move that grouchy hen again, and she attacked. She ruffled her feathers and flew at him. Henry yelled and stepped back, narrowly missing the lantern, and threw his arms up to block the hen. That action hurled the basket into the air, and the eggs plopped down on the ground, every one of them broken. The hen landed and pecked at Henry's shins. He grabbed the lantern and ran outside, slamming the door behind him.

He leaned against it, trying to catch his breath.

"Where are the eggs?" Rachel asked. She carried a bucket of milk toward the well house, where the milk from the night before was stored.

"I dropped the basket," Henry said in a rush. "A hen attacked me. I'm bleeding."

He thought Rachel would laugh at him, but instead she set down her bucket of milk and took the lantern from him and held it up.

"Where?"

He showed her, and she said, "Better go wash that off. Old Red caught you, didn't she? I didn't think to warn you about her. She's attacked me before, too."

Aunt Betsy said practically the same thing when she dressed the wounds on Henry's hand.

"I'm sorry," Henry told Uncle Andrew when he came in from the barn.

"It's no matter. There will be more eggs tomorrow before I go to town."

And there seemed no shortage of eggs for breakfast. Aunt Betsy and Mother fixed smoked ham, potatoes, eggs, biscuits, and ham gravy, and Henry ate his fill before Aunt Betsy packed extra food in Rachel's lunch bucket.

"Should I take some of my books to school?" Henry asked. He'd packed some of his favorites, although he didn't have his reader from school.

"Not today," Rachel said. "You can ask Mr. Carson if he wants you to bring them tomorrow."

"What's he like?" Louisa asked. "My teacher is a woman, and she's real nice. Does Mr. Carson whip you?"

Rachel laughed. "Not me, although he's cracked his stick on the knuckles of some of the older boys. He's fair. If you act right, he'll treat you right."

Henry had every intention of acting right, but how he wished he were back in Cincinnati walking to school with Raleigh instead of going to a place where he didn't know anyone except Rachel and Calvin.

There was no help for it, so he took the lunch pail from Rachel, and he, Louisa, Rachel, and Calvin set off for the one-room schoolhouse a couple miles down the road.

CHAPTER 10
The One-Room Schoolhouse

Louisa quizzed Rachel about the teacher and the students during the entire walk to school. Henry listened, and he had some questions of his own, but he couldn't get them in edgewise.

"There are a couple of girls your age and only one boy," Rachel said.

"How many are in this school?" Louisa asked.

"Seventeen."

Seventeen. Back in Cincinnati there were more than that in Henry's reader.

"It's right up there," Calvin said.

Above the autumn-colored leaves of the trees, Henry could see the peak of the belfry. A few minutes later they walked into the schoolyard. A couple of big boys were throwing rocks up in an oak tree, trying to knock something down, he figured, but he didn't stand around to watch. Instead he followed Rachel inside the small building.

She marched them to the front of the room where the teacher stood. He was a little man with a deep frown line between his eyes, and it got deeper when he looked at Henry and Louisa.

"New students?" he asked.

"Yes, sir," Rachel answered and made introductions.

"We don't know how long we'll be here," Henry explained. "When the cholera is gone, we'll go back to Cincinnati. Maybe next week," he said, but he knew that wasn't likely.

"I suspect there will be more who flee from town before you get to go back," Mr. Carson said. "Let me hear how you read." He had Louisa read from a book and then told her to sit next to Calvin.

"Your turn," he said and had Henry read a section. "You're very good." Mr. Carson had him read from a more advanced reader, then another. "Sit in the back by the older boys," he instructed him.

The older boys hadn't come in from outside, so Rachel showed Henry where they sat.

"Not there. That's Jeremiah's seat. Over here."

Henry slid onto a bench in the back as Mr. Carson pulled the bell rope. The clanging signal brought chattering students inside. A tall lanky boy of at least fifteen sat down by Henry. Another boy, this one burly, sat on his other side.

"Who are you, Shorty?" the tall boy said.

"Henry Lankford from Cincinnati."

"I think Shorty fits you better," he said.

"Are you Jeremiah?" Henry asked.

"You heard of me?"

"My cousin Rachel said you sat there."

"Rachel Farley's your cousin?" the boy on the other side asked.

Henry nodded and wasn't about to explain about being cousins several times removed.

"I'm David."

"What are you doing here, Shorty?" Jeremiah asked.

"I'm staying with Rachel until the cholera leaves town. And my name is Henry Lankford. I'm not short. I'm just not as old as you."

"Oh, yeah?" Jeremiah started to say something else, but the teacher tapped his long stick on his desk, commencing the school day.

Mr. Carson introduced Louisa and Henry, then he started different sections of the students on assignments. "David and Jeremiah fill up the wood box. Henry, bring in water," he ordered. Then he turned his attention back to the younger children and their sums.

Henry looked at Rachel with a question in his eyes. She pointed to the side of the room where a water bucket sat on a long table. Henry nodded his thanks and picked up the bucket and carried it outside. The other boys had already gone out to the woodpile. Henry glanced around for a well.

"Looking for something, Shorty?" Jeremiah asked.

Henry ignored him and walked toward the back of the schoolhouse. To the left sat the outhouse, and over by itself, a little distance to the right of the building, was the well.

Henry lowered the bucket that was tied to a rope and drew it back up. He poured the cold water into the schoolhouse bucket. He'd gotten it a little full, and some sloshed over the side onto his boot.

"Too heavy for you, Shorty?"

He wasn't surprised to hear Jeremiah's grating voice. Again he ignored him.

"How old are you, Shorty?" Jeremiah asked.

"I'll be eleven next week," Henry said.

"Eleven!" the boy exclaimed.

"How old are you?" Henry asked.

Jeremiah didn't answer.

"We're both fifteen," David said. He stood by the schoolhouse door with an armload of wood.

"So you *should* be bigger than me," Henry said, and before Jeremiah could respond, he pushed the door open and carried the bucket inside, being careful not to spill any water on the floor.

He took his seat and waited for Mr. Carson to give him more work. The other boys made another trip to the woodpile. It wasn't really cold outside because the early October sun shone brightly, but inside the schoolhouse the chill was more noticeable. Henry watched Jeremiah expertly add a log to the fire when he came back inside.

When Mr. Carson finally got to their part of the room, he gave them reading assignments and had them read to each other. Then he asked them to help the younger students with their reading. Henry immediately claimed Louisa and Calvin, and Mr. Carson nodded his approval.

At noon, the four cousins sat on the schoolhouse steps in the sun. Rachel pulled out some biscuits, cheese, and apples from her pail, and she handed out portions to her brother, Louisa, and Henry.

"Hurry and eat, and we'll go play prisoner's base with the others," she said.

Some of the other students had stayed inside to eat, and others, like Jeremiah and David, were also eating their meals outside. They must have downed their food in one gulp, for in no time they were organizing the game, with each of them being a team captain.

"I'll be on David's team," Henry said.

"You don't get to choose," Rachel said. "The captains choose their teams."

"At my school, we get to play with who we want to," Henry said.

"Well, this isn't your school," Rachel said. "And that's not how we do it here."

Henry finished his apple and got a drink from the well before sidling over to David's base area.

"Hey, Shorty, you're on my team," Jeremiah said before he could approach David.

"My name's Henry."

"Right, Shorty," Jeremiah said. He named off the others who were on their team.

Children of all ages darted every which way, running from members of the other team to keep from being tagged.

"Where's our territory?" Henry asked.

"Our base is the pine tree," Jeremiah said.

"But where's—"

"You're caught," David yelled as he tagged Henry on the back. "I'm taking you prisoner." He pushed him toward his team's base, the well.

"I don't even know the territories yet," Henry said. "You can't come in our safe area."

"We don't have safe areas," David said. He tugged on Henry's arm. "Come on."

"In Cincinnati we play this different. We have—"

"We're not in Cincinnati," David said. "Stay here until someone rescues you."

Henry stayed put. He'd thought of David as the nicer of the two older boys, but he wasn't playing fair.

Jeremiah darted to the well and slapped Henry's shoulder. "You're free. Run."

"Don't we have to count to ten before we run?"

"What? Run!" Jeremiah shouted.

Henry stood still with his hands on his hips. "But at my school, we—"

"This ain't your school," Jeremiah said. "Run!"

Rachel ran in and tagged Henry before he could take off. "You're still a prisoner," she yelled.

"You're not playing fair," Henry shouted. "In Cincinnati—"

"Time out!" Jeremiah yelled.

Everyone stopped, and all eyes turned toward Jeremiah, who marched over to Henry and stood toe to toe with him. Henry looked up over a foot to Jeremiah's face. Other students, including Rachel, moved behind an invisible line and stood on Jeremiah's side. Louisa edged toward Henry.

"This ain't Cincinnati," Jeremiah said. "If you want to play, you play by our rules."

Henry glanced at Rachel, who was staring steely-eyed at him.

"We play it differently," Henry said.

The group was silent, waiting for Jeremiah to react, but

he, too, remained silent.

"I suppose I could play by your rules, if you would explain them," Henry said. "Then if you come to my school in Cincinnati, I'll explain our rules." It was the best way he could weasel out of the situation.

Before the face-off could escalate, Mr. Carson rang the bell, calling the students back to class. Henry couldn't remember a more welcomed sound.

"This afternoon we'll have a spelling bee," the teacher announced.

"How can that be fair?" Henry whispered to David.

"Henry Lankford, do you want to say something to the school?" Mr. Carson asked in a gruff voice.

Henry gasped. He'd never been called down for talking in class before.

"Well?"

"I. . .I was wondering if the younger students would be given the same words as the older students."

Mr. Carson stared at him. "Of course not. The words will be according to the age of the speller." The teacher divided the students into two teams, and they lined up on opposite sides of the room.

"The first word is 'hat.' He wore a hat into the barn."

"H-a-t." The youngster spelled it correctly.

Mr. Carson turned to Henry's side of the room. He gave out words that fit the different abilities of the students. Then it was Henry's turn.

"Your word is 'quarantine.' The boy was placed in quarantine."

Henry pronounced the word, then spelled it correctly. It didn't hurt that he'd seen that word over and over in Dr.

Drake's medical journals.

Mr. Carson went through the students again. A few misspelled their words and had to take their seats. Henry's next word was "embargo." He spelled it successfully.

Within a few minutes, there were only three students left. Jeremiah and Rachel on one side of the room faced Henry on the other side.

Rachel missed "desert" by putting in an extra "s," which made it "dessert," and she had to sit down.

"Your word is 'monthly.' The moon is full monthly."

Henry spelled it right.

"Jeremiah, your word is 'renowned.' He was a renowned writer."

"Renowned. R-e-n-o-u-n-e-d."

"That's incorrect. Henry, spell 'renowned.' He was a renowned writer."

"Renowned. R-e-n-o-w-n-e-d."

"Correct," Mr. Carson said. "You may both be seated."

The teacher didn't say one word to Henry about being the winning speller. Instead he started a geography lesson for all of the students.

"I think we'll change Shorty's name to 'Smartypants,'" Jeremiah whispered to David in a voice loud enough for Henry to hear. Mr. Carson didn't call him down.

Henry preferred Shorty. By the end of the day, he had had enough of the country school, but Mr. Carson wasn't through with him.

"Henry, you can take your turn today sweeping out the schoolroom."

Henry looked at Rachel, who only smirked at him and lifted her eyebrows in an innocent way.

"Yes, sir." After school was dismissed, Henry swept out the place.

"You're a very smart boy," Mr. Carson said when he was finished. "But you need to learn to adapt to your situation."

"What do you mean, sir?" Henry asked.

"You're smart enough. I'm sure you'll figure it out before tomorrow."

Henry put on his coat and went outside. How he wished he were back in Cincinnati, walking home from school with Raleigh. Back home. What was going on there today? How many people had died?

Henry walked down the road by himself. It wasn't until he rounded a big curve that blocked the schoolhouse from view that he saw Rachel standing at the side of the road.

"Where's Louisa?" he asked.

"She and Calvin went on home." Rachel fell in step with him.

"Why'd you wait? I thought you were on the side against me."

"There shouldn't be a side against you. Why'd you act like a big know-it-all from Cincinnati?"

"I'm a know-it-all just because I know how to spell?" What did she expect from him anyway? Was he supposed to forget everything he'd already learned at school?

"We do things different in the country. You should do them our way when you're here. You expect me to do things your way when I'm in town."

"Yes, but you don't. You were rude to Dr. Drake. You the same as called him a grave robber."

"Well, he dug up an Indian mound, which is a grave. What do you call that?"

Henry was silent. He had no answer to that question. He could see both sides of the question. Dr. Drake wanted to preserve historical artifacts, and Rachel didn't want people bothering an Indian grave.

An unspoken truce stretched between the two cousins. When they got home, they walked to the creek and measured the depth. There was no change. As a matter of habit, Henry also recorded the cloud formations and looked at the weathervane on the barn for the wind direction. But he had one more thing to say about the day's experiences before he could let it go.

"I don't like Jeremiah. When Mr. Carson was busy at the other side of the room, he called me Smartypants," he told Rachel as they walked back from the creek.

"Smartypants!" she said.

"Smartypants! Smartypants!" the crow on her shoulders echoed.

"Well, you are pretty smart." She looked at his trousers. "I don't know that your pants are smart, though," she said and laughed.

"That's not funny," Henry said. "I hate that school. It's so little."

Rachel glared at him. "It doesn't have to be big because there aren't very many of us around here. We live on large farms instead of close together like townspeople."

Once again, she was right, so Henry said nothing.

The next day, Henry collected the eggs, except for the one under Old Red. He let Uncle Andrew get that one before he took off for market. This time, Uncle Andrew didn't take his family with him. He went into Cincinnati alone.

Henry trudged to school with the others. It wasn't as bad

as the first day because he knew what to expect. He didn't argue about rules. He didn't even play the games. He stayed to himself and watched.

Later that afternoon when Uncle Andrew returned, he wasn't alone. Miss Emma Broadrick sat on the high bench of the wagon beside him.

Henry was outside when they drove up.

"Miss Emma?" he said with a question in his voice.

"Hannah died of cholera," she said and broke into tears.

CHAPTER 11
Rachel's Secret

After Miss Emma's announcement, Henry ran behind the henhouse and cried. He sobbed for Miss Hannah, who had always been kind to him. When he returned to the house, the family was grouped around Miss Emma as she sat in the parlor. She was still sniffling. Mother's eyes were red, and Rachel had tears on her cheeks.

"Can you talk now?" Mother asked as she patted Miss Emma's hand. "When did this happen?"

"Monday evening. That morning a peddler came around

selling apples. Hannah's been wanting fruit, so she asked me to get her some and I did. She wasn't strong at all, and after she ate the apple, which was a little on the green side, the cholera attacked her. She died before sunset."

"Does George know?" Mother asked.

"Oh, yes. I sent for him straight away when she got sick. He brought Dr. Drake, but it was too late to move Hannah to the pesthouse. We buried her yesterday. George thought I should come out here, and Andrew brought me." Miss Emma glanced at him with grateful eyes.

"Well, you're welcome to stay here as long as you'd like," Aunt Betsy said. "I think we should have a service for Miss Hannah before we have our meal. Andrew?"

"It would only be fitting," he said. While he got the family Bible from a parlor table, Aunt Betsy fetched her violin from the bedroom.

She played a hymn, then Uncle Andrew talked about the blessings of God and the glory of life in the hereafter, where Miss Hannah now resided. Mother spoke about Miss Hannah's goodness, and Aunt Betsy remembered times when she was young and Miss Hannah had helped her with sewing.

"I'm sorry my children didn't know Miss Hannah well," Aunt Betsy said. "If we had lived in Cincinnati, they would have been good friends."

"I helped with the flood cleanup," Rachel said. "She was nice to me then."

"She always talked to me at church," Louisa said. "And she gave me the chicken leg when she'd have Sunday dinner with us."

"She was always generous," Miss Emma said with a sniff.

"Henry?" Mother prodded him.

He didn't know what to say. He had so many memories of the wonderful old lady. "When we found snakes in the cellar, but we couldn't tell if we'd gotten them all out because the water was high down there, she said it was okay that I didn't tell Miss Emma, but that she was glad I told her so she could keep an eye out for it."

"There was another snake!" Miss Emma exclaimed. "Why didn't she tell me?"

Miss Emma sounded so much like her old self when she used to argue with Miss Hannah that Henry couldn't help but laugh out loud.

Once he started, he couldn't stop laughing. It was a laughter of relief. Mother joined in, and then the others. Miss Emma's loud laugh sounded almost natural. After the laughter died down, Henry felt better, almost as if Miss Hannah was still among them.

"Miss Hannah's probably looking down here today and laughing with us," Aunt Betsy said.

Uncle Andrew read a verse from the Bible about ashes to ashes and dust to dust, the family prayed together, and then the service was over.

"When we go back to Cincinnati, you must show me where she's buried so I can put flowers on her grave," Mother said.

"I will," Miss Emma said, and she almost teared up again, but she blinked and walked to the kitchen with her head high and offered to help Aunt Betsy with supper.

Henry held back and touched Mother on the arm to get her attention.

"Do you think Father will be all right?"

"Don't worry, Son. He'll be fine," she said with that tight

smile of hers that told him she only half-believed her own words. "We'll keep praying for him."

The next morning, Henry waited until Rachel was through with the milking before he gathered the eggs. He collected the ones in all the nests but Old Red's and watched as Rachel clucked at the hen and sneaked her hand to the side of the chicken before reaching under her and getting the egg.

"There's a special way," she said. "You want to do the milking while I get the eggs? I only milk Short Ears."

"Short Ears?"

"When she was a calf, the tips of her ears got froze off one winter. We give all our cows names that fit them. There's old Muley. Papa milks her because she has a mind of her own. And there's Roany, because her hide is sprinkled with white hairs."

"Well, it doesn't matter what their names are. I've never milked a cow. You'd have to show me."

Rachel laughed. "Tonight I'll teach you how to milk," she said.

School that day was easier than the other two days. Henry didn't react when the others called him Smartypants, so they quit doing it.

When he finished doing his sums and was waiting for the teacher to give him something else to do, Henry made a list of cholera symptoms. He wrote it on one of the sheets of paper he reserved for his observations. It was important that he make this list for Father. After all, Henry had read everything Dr. Drake had given him about cholera, and he knew Father hadn't had the extra time to read all the medical magazines.

Cholera Symptoms
1. diarrhea
2. vomiting
3. stomach cramps
4. blue skin
5. cold hands and feet

Those were all the symptoms he could recall. He stuck the paper in the pocket of his trousers, and after school, when he got to Rachel's house, he asked Miss Emma if he could talk to her.

"I want to know more about cholera," he said.

"Why?" she asked, and he could see the look in her eye that said she didn't want to talk about it.

"I want to give a list of symptoms to Father."

She heaved a deep sigh. "It's a nasty disease, and I can't think of where Hannah got it except from that apple she ate."

"That's probably it," Henry said. "Dr. Drake told me the disease is carried by invisible poisonous insects, sort of like gnats, but we can't see them. You know how gnats buzz around overripe apples? Maybe the cholera insects fly around not quite ripe apples."

"Maybe so," she said and looked thoughtfully into space, then turned her gaze to Henry. "First Hannah got diarrhea real bad. Then she got to vomiting. Her stomach hurt her so much. It was like she was poisoned."

"Did her skin turn blue?" Henry asked.

"Near the end it did. How do you know so much about this?"

"I've read Dr. Drake's medical magazines. Were her hands cold?"

"Near to freezing. She couldn't get them warm—her feet neither. I put hot bricks in bed with her, but they didn't help." A tear rolled down her lined face. "I couldn't do anything to help her."

Henry was at a loss to know what to do to comfort Miss Emma. He patted her hand and told her he appreciated her telling him so he could warn Father.

"It's a filthy disease," Miss Emma said. "Some say it's punishment coming from God's own hand, but why would he punish my Hannah?"

"I don't think it's God's punishment," Henry said. That was the first time he'd said it out loud, but he had been thinking about it ever since the preacher had brought up the idea that the drunks down in the shantytown were getting sick because of their sin.

"If you get the disease, it's because the invisible insects got to you," Henry said, "not because God wants to strike you dead. He couldn't have picked out Miss Hannah. The insects got her."

"Dr. Drake said since she was already feeling poorly, she was weak and an easy target for cholera. I don't rightly understand it, Henry," Miss Emma said.

He nodded. He didn't rightly understand it either, no matter how he tried.

That evening, Henry tried his hand at milking, but all he did was provide Rachel with a good belly laugh. He tried different ways of pulling on the teats, but he couldn't get so much as a drop of milk out.

"You pull and squeeze at the same time," Rachel said. "There's a rhythm to it." She sat down on the three-legged stool and showed him one more time. The warm milk made a *ping-ping* sound as it hit the side of the bucket.

Again, Henry took the place on the stool and tried it. He pulled. He squeezed. Short Ears bawled. Then she kicked her hind leg out, scaring Henry so much he tipped over the pail, spilling the milk that Rachel already had gotten in the bucket.

"I guess I'll go back to collecting the eggs," Henry said, and Rachel held her stomach because she laughed so hard. Her action reminded Henry of one of the symptoms of cholera, and he choked back a sob for his father, who was living in the midst of the epidemic.

On Sunday Father arrived not long after sunup. After breakfast, the families rode in the wagon to the schoolhouse, where a traveling preacher talked about the wrath of God that had descended on Cincinnati and the curse on the immoral and ungodly.

Henry and Miss Emma exchanged a glance, and he shook his head. She stared belligerently at the preacher. Father, who sat beside Henry, patted his arm and whispered, "We'll talk later."

It was after Sunday dinner that Father asked Henry to walk with him for a while. They walked down to the creek, and Henry showed Father where he and Rachel measured the height of the water.

"Dr. Drake sends a message," Father said. "He sees no evidence that the vicious and poverty-stricken and drunkards are more liable to the disease than temperate people who never take a drink of alcohol. He didn't want you thinking that Miss Hannah was taking a nip now and then."

"I didn't think that. I think anyone that the insects attack is going to get it." Henry dug in his trousers' pocket for his list. "Here are the symptoms. At the first sign, you must run to Dr. Drake. At the first sign!" Henry repeated. "I remember reading that half the people who get cholera will die. The other half, if they can be treated in time, will live. At the first sign, you must be treated!"

"How old are you?" Father asked with a smile.

"Eleven on Tuesday," Henry answered.

"I'm not so sure. Sometimes I think you're older than me," he said. "You sound like my father." He reached over and tousled Henry's blond hair. "We'd better get back to the others."

They sat in the yard on chairs and quilts, taking advantage of the late September sunshine until time for Father to return to Cincinnati. Mother held his hand as he mounted his horse for the ride back to town.

Henry stood nearby and overheard her ask "How many have died?"

"Over a hundred fifty this week," he said. "But don't worry about me. I'll be fine." He bent down and kissed Mother, and again she watched until he was out of sight.

Henry looked around for Rachel, but she was nowhere to be seen. He figured she was down by the creek. In the last few days, he had seen her head that direction when they'd already measured the creek depth.

With an hour before sunset, he decided to explore the creek himself. Rachel had always guided him to the spot with the giant chestnut tree, but he wanted to look upstream. He told Mother where he was going, and she nodded absently and looked down the road where Father had disappeared.

Henry followed the route he and Louisa had gone on their first day at the farm. He came to the ford in the creek, where stepping rocks stuck out of the water. He'd cross there and look at the creek from a different angle on the other side. With care, he balanced on the rocks and made it across without even getting the toes of his boots wet. On this side of the creek he saw deer tracks. Or at least that's what he thought they would be. They were hoof prints much smaller than a horse's. But they were oddly spaced. Three made deeper imprints in the soft creek bank than the other one. Odd.

Cautiously, he made his way along the bank. This was obviously a drinking hole for the deer. Perhaps there were other wild animals about.

He had gone only a hundred yards upstream when he heard Rachel's pet crow's shrill caw. "Good boy. Good boy," Echo said, and Henry knew Rachel couldn't be far away.

Still, he proceeded quietly. He didn't know what she did down here by the creek. He'd never asked her or even told her he'd seen her come this way, and she'd never let on that she came down here without him.

He slipped back in the brush, away from the creek bank, and circled toward the sound he'd heard. As he got closer to her, he could hear her croon softly.

"Good boy. Now hold still, little fellow."

"Good boy," the crow mimicked.

Henry crouched behind a clump of bramble bushes and gingerly pushed a prickly branch out of the way so he could see her.

"That's it," she said. "Let me get a good look. We might take this off today, little fellow."

She was bending over a young fawn, her arms encircling its head to hold it still, but her hands reaching down to touch its leg. Wooden splints were wrapped tightly with twine.

"Rachel," he said in a soft voice so that he wouldn't disturb the deer.

Her head shot up, but she didn't let go of the deer. It struggled in her grasp, evidently alarmed by her behavior.

"Go away," she said in a low voice, but one that said she meant it.

"I'll help you," he said and quickly let go of the bramble branch, which pricked his finger. He stuck it in his mouth and sucked on it for a second as he came out from behind the bush.

"When did he break his leg?"

"Go away," she repeated in that low voice so she wouldn't upset the deer.

"I can hold him for you so you can take the splint off. Has it been on long enough?"

"I can take care of him," she said. "Good boy. Hold still." The deer stomped a hoof.

Henry advanced one slow step at a time. When he got beside her he asked, "Where do you want me to hold him?"

"All right," she said, giving in. "Pet him on his hind end, then slowly grab his back feet, and we'll lay him down. Then hold him tight while I cut this twine."

Henry saw a butcher knife lying on the ground nearby.

"This could hurt him."

"I know, but it's time. Now! Turn him."

Henry was practically sitting on the animal, holding him down.

Rachel knelt in front of him, petting him and crooning softly. She waited until the deer had settled down. Then she reached for the knife. With a swift, deft movement she cut the knot. The fawn reared, but Henry held on tight and calmed him until Rachel could unwind the twine and release the crude splints. She felt the leg and moved it gently back and forth.

"Feels strong. Let him up."

Henry jumped back, and the deer sprang to its feet. It favored the broken leg but darted back into the underbrush and away.

"Why didn't you tell me?" he asked.

"Why should I?" she said and turned on him like a wounded animal. "You always talk about being a doctor and about how everyone can be what he wants to be in this great country. Well, not everybody can. I want to be a doctor for animals. Do you think that's likely for a girl?"

CHAPTER 12

Rachel's Hospital

After her outburst, Rachel stormed off. Henry retraced his steps to the crossing rocks and walked back to the house, but she hadn't returned. What could he say to Rachel when he found her anyway?

Were there women who took care of animals? He'd never heard of one. Could they be strong enough? Rachel had obviously wrestled the fawn to be able to put that splint on it in the first place. And whoever heard of fixing a broken leg on a deer? They sure didn't fix horses' legs or cows' legs. They shot the animals and put them out of their misery.

But that wouldn't be Rachel's way. She had insisted they

return the flood-trapped snakes to the Ohio River. She would try to save any animal.

It was almost dark. Surely Rachel would come back soon. He didn't want to ask Aunt Betsy about her because he didn't want to get Rachel in trouble if she wasn't allowed to stay down at the creek this late.

He was about to put on his nightshirt when he heard the kitchen door open and shut. It had to be her. He slipped out of the front bedroom and through the parlor, where the adults were still talking.

"I need a drink of water," he told them as he strolled through the room to the kitchen.

It was her all right. He walked over to the water bucket and lowered the dipper and drank the water, never letting his eyes leave hers. He hung the dipper back on the rim of the bucket.

"No, I have never heard of a girl being an animal doctor." He answered her earlier question as if she'd just asked it instead of an hour having passed since they last spoke. He continued in the same low voice so the adults wouldn't hear. "But that doesn't mean you can't be the first. How did you get that splint on the deer anyway? Did you have help?"

She took her turn at the water bucket, then faced him.

"I knocked him out with a rock."

"You hit the deer?"

"What else could I do? He was in bad pain. I figured if I killed him, it would be better than what he was going through, but if it just knocked him out, maybe I could fix him up. He was already down." She said it as if she hadn't wanted to hurt him but didn't have a choice.

"They shoot horses that break their legs," Henry said.

"I know, but I thought even if he died, I could work on the leg and learn about it. I ran up here and got the supplies I'd need, then I clunked him with a big rock. Once I saw that he was still breathing, I put the splint on. I didn't know if I got the bone in the right place, but it felt right. I stayed with him until he woke up, and I gave him water and some grain. He trusted me, but when I left him that night, I didn't know if he'd be gone or worse—dead—when I went back the next day."

A memory clicked in his mind. "That's why you wanted that book on bones from the library, isn't it?"

"That was before I found the deer. I wanted the book to see if I'd fixed a rabbit's broken foot right. It had been caught in a trap. It ran away, and I haven't seen it since."

"You need to be getting to bed," Aunt Betsy called from the parlor.

"Yes, Mama, we're going."

"Rachel, why can't you be an animal doctor?" Henry asked in a quick whisper. "You sure enough like animals. You fixed up Echo."

"He was easy. I just caught worms and fed him milk until he was strong enough to fly away. Trouble is, he didn't want to fly off. He just stayed around. I guess he likes me," she said with a tinge of pride in her voice.

"Let's ask Dr. Drake about it. He'll know how to go about becoming an animal doctor." A thought occurred to him. "Have you asked Aunt Betsy about it?"

"No. I can't think she'd want me to be something I shouldn't be. She'd say it was man's work. I don't know why fixing up animals would be much different from fixing up people."

She had a point, as she usually did. The way Aunt Betsy and Uncle Andrew had Rachel help at market instead of being in school, as if it wasn't important to be there, made him think she was probably right about their attitudes. But you could never tell with adults.

"We'll talk to Dr. Drake about it," he said again. "Whenever we can get back to Cincinnati."

He wondered what Mother would think of this. And would Miss Emma have any knowledge of things like this? She had never married and had a family like Mother, but somehow he doubted that she'd ever wanted to do anything outside of taking care of a house. Now Miss Hannah—she was a different story. If it were possible, she probably wanted to do it. For such a frail woman, she had a strong backbone. For a moment he'd forgotten that she was dead from cholera. When he remembered, he felt a welling up from inside that made it hard to swallow.

"We'd better get to bed," he said in a low voice.

"Yes, but tomorrow after school, I'll show you something I've been working on."

"What?" he asked.

"Tomorrow," she said and walked toward the stairs.

The next day it seemed the teacher would never let school out. The walk home seemed longer than normal, too. When they could finally see Rachel's house, he broke into a run until he realized it wouldn't do any good for him to get home any faster than Rachel, and she was just poking along with Louisa and Calvin.

What could her surprise possibly be, anyway? He knew why she went to the creek—to see the deer. He could account

115

for her whereabouts all the other times, so what could she be working on?

"We're going to go measure the creek, Mama," Rachel said when they walked in the door. She put the lunch pail in the kitchen and walked out the back door with Henry on her heels. Echo flew from the barn roof and landed on her shoulder.

They hurried to the creek and really did measure the water, which was up a little bit from rain in the night.

"This can't be the surprise," Henry said. "I've known about your measuring notch on the tree trunk since the first day I came."

"Follow me," she said. They went farther upstream to the rocks, crossed the creek, then continued along the bank, past the place where Henry had found her with the deer.

"Here," she said with a sweep of her hand.

"Here. Here," the crow on her shoulder mimicked.

Henry looked around. What was this? There were crates and coops of various sizes, all rather crudely built and all extending to the edge of the water.

"This is my hospital," she said. "An animal hospital. Over here I have. . .Well, come see."

She led him to the first coop. It held several curled up young foxes.

"They're orphans," she said. "The mother was probably shot for raiding henhouses. Anyway, when I found them, I didn't touch them for two days, waiting for her to come back. She never came."

"What do you feed foxes?"

"That's a problem. I don't have any dead chickens, so I've been giving them eggs. I have their pen partly in the water so they can get a drink whenever they want."

Henry reached in to pet one.

"Oh, you can't treat them like kittens, even though they might look like them. They're wild, and they have to be able to return to the wild when they're big enough."

Henry jerked back. "When will that be?"

"Another couple weeks. Over here," she said and waved her hand, "is a rabbit. It was also caught in a trap, but it didn't die. I don't know who's setting traps on our land. I get rid of them when I find them."

"Why don't these animals bite you when you put a splint on them? Did you knock this one out, too?"

"It's the only way I know how to help them."

"Have you killed any?"

"A possum never did wake up."

"You sure it wasn't fooling you?" Henry said with a laugh. "Playing possum on you?"

"He was dead. There was no heartbeat. I made sure before I cut him open."

Henry's mouth flew open, and he left the rabbit crate and faced Rachel.

"You cut him open?"

"Like Dr. Drake said about the skeleton in his office. That's how you learn about the parts."

Henry looked around. "Where's the skeleton?"

"Over here." She lifted a solid crate that was high on the bank, not near the water. "I had to boil him to get the meat off like you would a pig's head to make head cheese. I was careful not to disturb any of the bones, but they came apart because there weren't any muscles left. It was like boiling a chicken. I should have known that."

Henry looked at the skeleton with great interest. Rachel had tied the bones together with twine and in places she'd used nails. It didn't look exactly like a possum, but she'd done a pretty good job.

"Do you think animal doctors ever operate on animals? I mean, they're not like people."

"Oh, I know, but I thought it would help to see the bones."

"Probably animal doctors give animal medicine to the sick ones."

"Or the same medicine. I heard Papa say that cholera doctors in Cincinnati are giving calomel to children in amounts that were fit for a horse."

Henry caught his breath. No matter what he did, no matter how far removed he thought he was from cholera, it kept coming back to him. He wondered if his friend Raleigh was sick. He closed his eyes and said a silent prayer, asking for Raleigh to be healthy.

"You all right?"

"I'm fine. So, you have the foxes and a rabbit. That's all?"

"That's all right now," she said. "I could have more tomorrow. It depends on what I find that's hurt."

The next day on the road to school, they found a hawk that was riddled with buckshot.

"Somebody missed a clean shot, I suspect," Rachel said. "It could only fly this far before falling."

They didn't have to knock the bird out, because it was already lying down, barely breathing. It didn't put up a fight when Rachel picked it up.

"What can you do for it?" Henry asked.

"I don't know, but I'll take it home after school and give it some water."

She placed it under a tree near the schoolyard, and when

noon arrived, she and Henry went out to look at the bird. It was already dead.

"Will you cut it up?" Henry asked.

Rachel shook her head and didn't answer for a moment. "It's too much like a chicken, and I know what they look like inside."

It didn't seem right to leave it there under the tree. Henry found a stout stick and dug a hole in the ground where it was fairly soft. Rachel placed the bird in the shallow grave, and together they covered it with dirt. There weren't any flowers around to decorate the grave, but the sumac leaves had already turned brilliant red, so they picked a few stems and planted them in the dirt.

"Should we say some words over him?" Henry asked.

"Ashes to ashes, dust to dust," Rachel used the same words that her father had said in their memorial service for Miss Hannah. "Do you think animals go to heaven?"

"I don't know," Henry said. "I don't know about that."

That night, they had birthday cake with supper, and the others called out "Happy Birthday" to Henry.

"Your father is sorry he couldn't be here, but he sends his love and this," Mother said. She handed him a book. "It's one that Dr. Drake recommended. Happy Birthday."

Henry leafed through the medical dictionary. "It's perfect," he said. "Thank you, Mother."

Later that evening before bed, he read the inscription in the front. "To my son, who will someday be a great doctor because he cares about people. I carry your list with me. With love, Father."

The next morning, Uncle Andrew headed to town for market day, but he returned early that afternoon, right as

Henry and the others got home from school.

He wore a solemn expression, and he pulled the rig up in front of the house, instead of driving it to the barn.

"Rachel," he called, and she and Henry ran up to him. "Put the team up for me."

"Papa, what's wrong?" she asked.

"I need to talk to your mother," he said and climbed down from the wagon, handing her the reins.

Henry climbed onboard with Rachel, and she drove the team to the barn and parked the wagon. He helped her unhitch the horses, and while they drank greedily from the water trough, he and Rachel brushed them down.

Rachel kept glancing toward the house.

"Something's wrong," she said. "Something's bad wrong."

Henry's heart was in his throat as he thought of his father in Cincinnati with the cholera insects. But if Father was sick, wouldn't Uncle Andrew have said he needed to talk to Mother?

As soon as they put the horses in their stalls, Henry and Rachel ran for the house. They burst into the kitchen, but no one was there. They found everyone in the parlor, sitting in stunned silence. Uncle Andrew hugged Aunt Betsy, who looked pale and had tears streaming down her cheeks.

"Who died?" Henry asked in a tight voice.

"Richard Allerton," Uncle Andrew answered. "The funeral was this morning. His brother Ben came to the market to get me. Richard had sent his family away. They don't know he's dead."

Aunt Betsy sobbed, and Uncle Andrew held her head against his chest.

Henry sat down on the floor. Father could be dead, and

they wouldn't know it for days. That lump that kept welling up into his throat was back, nearly choking him.

Rachel walked into the bedroom and returned with her mother's violin, the violin that Richard had given her. They had played music together at the Independence Day picnic in Henry's yard.

Rachel handed the violin to her mother. "I think he would want you to play a hymn for him," she said.

CHAPTER 13
Henry's Worst Fear

"Please don't go back on market day," Aunt Betsy said to Uncle Andrew at the supper table that night. "You might never return."

"Could we talk about this later?" he asked and gave a slight nod toward Henry and the others.

"Yes, I'm sorry," Aunt Betsy said quickly. "More potatoes, Miss Emma?" she said in a falsely bright voice.

Henry stole a look at Mother, who sat in a rigid position next to him. She'd been very quiet after the service they'd held for Richard. She wasn't crying. She just stared into space as if she wasn't seeing anything.

Henry felt as if he could barely breathe. First Miss Hannah had died, and now Richard. Mother had explained how Miss Hannah was old and frail and easily succumbed to cholera. But Richard? He had been a strong man. Strong, like Father.

The families were quiet that October night, and they all went to bed earlier than usual. But Henry lay awake long into the dark, and he heard his mother restlessly fight the quilts on the bed beside him.

Morning started in the same way as always. Henry collected eggs, and Rachel milked the cows with her father. The children went to school. But nothing was the same for Henry until Sunday morning, when Father rode into the yard.

He released a pent-up breath he didn't know he'd been holding. It was as if his whole body had been bound up like that deer's leg in the splint. He felt as if the twine that bound it had been cut, and he was free again.

Mother rushed outside as soon as they heard the horse's hooves. She embraced Father in the front yard. They came inside, and Father hugged Henry and Louisa.

"I'm so glad you're here," Mother said. "Come tell us the news."

"Good morning," Father said to the others who were gathered in the parlor. "Andrew, I knew Betsy had tied you up when you didn't come to town yesterday."

"Just about," Andrew said with a slow grin. "She's got a pretty good grip on me."

"It's just as well. Half the people have left town."

"Then can you stay, too?" Mother asked.

He looked at her and shook his head no. "We have an order for this steamboat we're working on, and we need to finish it. I gave my word."

"But your life. . ." Mother said, then stopped herself and gave that tight smile that Henry was getting used to.

There was no preacher at church at the little schoolhouse that Sunday. He only came every other week. Instead of hearing preaching, the folks sang hymns and then held a prayer circle. Young and old held hands, and each person said a prayer as his or her turn came.

"Thank You for this good day," Mother said, "and please keep my husband safe."

"Thank You for this day, and please let Father not catch cholera," Louisa said next.

"Thank You for this day and for Your Son, and please stop the cholera from killing any more people," Aunt Betsy said.

And it was the same as the prayer made the circle. Cholera was at the front of everyone's mind.

"Have you seen Raleigh?" Henry asked over Sunday dinner.

"He and his family are visiting his grandparents," Father said. "He's fine."

Henry said a silent prayer of thanks.

"What about the preacher?" Mother asked.

"He left town, too. Like I said, half the town's gone."

"What about Dr. Drake?" Henry asked.

"He's got his hands full with patients. Only help he can get at the hospital is from the Sisters of Charity. Anyone who visits gets pressed into service. Even me, and what do I know about nursing?" he asked.

"Why were you at the hospital?" Mother asked.

Father hesitated. "John Hanks died."

Henry drew a deep breath. One of the men at Father's shipyard—dead.

"It's not contagious," he quickly assured Mother. "Dr. Drake says so."

"I know," Mother said and smiled that tight smile again.

Too soon it was time for Father to go back to Cincinnati. Henry and Rachel brought the horse around, and Henry held it for Father as he and Mother walked arm in arm.

"If you get sick, send someone to tell me. Richard's family still doesn't know," she said.

"I won't get sick," Father said.

"I know you won't," she said, "but promise me."

"I promise. But don't you worry." He kissed her on the forehead and hugged her tight.

"How many?" Mother asked. "How many have died?"

Father hesitated. "Dr. Drake says around four hundred."

"In two weeks!" Mother exclaimed.

"Father, you have my list?" Henry asked, referring to his list of cholera symptoms.

"I have your list," Father said.

"At the first sign—"

"I know," Father interrupted him, and Henry figured he didn't want to talk more about cholera. "I'll see you next Sunday." He kissed Mother again and climbed on his horse.

The days fell into a pattern. Up early to do chores, to school, to the creek to measure the water and check on the animals, to bed, up early to do chores. Midweek market day came and went, with Uncle Andrew staying on the farm.

"It's a good day to dig sprouts out of the pasture," he told Henry. "Can't have our best milkers tripping over sprouts."

Henry stared at him. Whoever heard of cows tripping on

tree sprouts? He knew Uncle Andrew was making an excuse for not going to market. He didn't want to go where the cholera was.

The awful grip on Henry's heart that had come back when Father rode off to town got tighter and tighter as each day passed.

By Thursday he was having a hard time getting from one minute to the next. Miss Hannah, dead. Richard, dead. John Hanks, dead. And who else could cholera have claimed by now?

He dragged his feet walking home from school. He could barely eat supper. The food that he forced down could have been sawdust for all that he noticed.

On Friday morning he gathered the eggs and walked with the others to school. He walked with a rhythm. Left foot, right foot. Every step seemed to pound in his brain the words "two days." Two days. Two days until Father came back safe. Two days.

School was easier because the boys called him Henry now. He still stayed to himself, but it didn't matter anymore. Nothing seemed to matter.

After school he walked aimlessly down to the creek, more out of habit than out of any desire to measure the height of the water. Rachel rambled on about seeing the deer yesterday and how it was running just as if it had never broken its leg. She talked about the rabbit. She talked and she talked.

"Come on, slowpoke," Rachel called as she ran ahead of him to the partly submerged notched tree. She recorded the depth of the water.

"Slowpoke. Slowpoke," her pesky crow said.

"Leave me alone," Henry answered. He was tired of that crow. He was tired of measuring the water. It didn't make any difference. It didn't make the cholera go away. It didn't prove anything.

"I wonder if we should let the foxes go today? They're getting bigger, and I want them to—"

"Shut up," Henry yelled at her. "I don't care about your animals. They're just dumb animals. They don't matter." He saw the shock in her eyes, and her mouth fell open. She stepped toward him.

"What's wrong with you? They are not dumb animals," she shouted back at him.

"Yes, they are. They are." Screaming felt good to Henry, and he screamed into her face. "They don't matter. They're not people. They're not dying." Tears flooded his eyes, but he didn't care. "They don't matter," he yelled again as tears ran down his cheeks.

"Cry baby," Rachel shouted.

"Cry baby. Cry baby," Echo said in his bird voice.

Rachel ran ahead toward the crossing rocks, and Henry fell to his knees on the banks of the creek. He had never felt so out of control in his life. Fear had overcome him. He felt as if he were a hundred years old instead of eleven.

"Father, please come back. Please." He sobbed. "Father." After awhile, he sat up and looked around. Everything was the same as before he had indulged in the shouting match with Rachel. Everything was the same, yet everything was different. He knew he had hurt Rachel, and he really hadn't meant to. It wasn't her fault that cholera made him be in the country instead of in town, where he should be in his own home. It wasn't her fault that Father stayed in town to work.

It wasn't her fault that people he knew were dying.

He walked downstream. He hadn't gone past the measuring tree before. Instead of dried cornstalks in rows, he could look through the brush that grew along the creek bank and see cows grazing in the pasture. He heard Uncle Andrew call the cows in for the evening milking, and he watched them amble toward the milk barn. In the distance he saw the Indian burial mound that Rachel had told him about. Even out here was a reminder of death.

He knew he had to go back. It was getting colder as the sun got lower in the sky, and his coat didn't keep out the October wind. But he walked a little farther until he couldn't see the house, couldn't see the big barn or the outbuildings. Dusk had fallen when he finally turned around and started back.

"Henry," he heard Rachel's voice calling when he neared their measuring tree.

"I'm here," he said in a flat voice.

He walked on toward the tree, and he heard her footsteps in the brush as she approached him.

"I'm sorry," she said.

That surprised him. Wasn't he the one who had told her that her animals were dumb?

"Why?"

"Mama says you are fearful, and you must turn your trust back to God. She says you need understanding, not me calling you a cry baby. What if it were my papa in Cincinnati? How would I feel? I'd be crying all the time, that's how I'd feel. Are you scared, Henry?"

Henry swallowed. He and Rachel had been through a lot. They'd captured snakes together in the flooded house. They'd learned about medical things. She'd confided about her dream of being an animal doctor, and he'd told her about wanting to be a doctor. She didn't like the town that much, but he wasn't crazy about the country, either. They were different, and they were the same. He should trust her with his feelings and know she wouldn't laugh at him.

"I'm scared," he confessed.

"It's all right, Henry. But you have to turn your fear over to God. Mama says that will lighten your burden."

Henry bowed his head. "Dear God, please take my fear away," he prayed. "Amen."

"Amen," Rachel repeated. "Let's go back home. We've already eaten supper, but Mama saved you some beans and cornbread."

Henry walked beside Rachel, and he felt his burden lift. He could do nothing about what was going on in Cincinnati. He had to have faith that God would take care of him.

When they walked in the kitchen door, Mother held out her arms to Henry. She held him tight and kissed the top of his head.

"You should be a carefree boy," she said. "But you're a young man already." She stepped back. "You must be hungry." Henry knew Aunt Betsy must have talked to Mother, but she didn't ask where he'd been, so he didn't explain.

After a bowl of beans, Henry went to bed with a lighter heart.

Saturday dawned clear and bright, but with an October chill in the air.

"I'm sorry about calling your animals dumb," Henry said as he and Rachel walked down to the creek.

"That's okay. They aren't important like people dying,

but that doesn't mean I want to help them any less."

Rachel recorded the creek depth, and Henry looked up at the bright blue sky.

"No clouds. Rachel, how can cholera be spread by bad atmosphere when it's such a clear, sunny day?"

She stared at the sky.

"Maybe it's not so clear in Cincinnati."

"It's only seven miles away. We should be able to see seven miles in the sky, shouldn't we? I wish we could go to the library and find that book about clouds. I wish we could ask Dr. Drake what he thinks about this."

He caught himself. Wishing was better than fearing things, but he needed to turn his thoughts in a different direction. "Let's check on the animals."

They turned the foxes loose that day. Together they lifted the coop off the curled-up foxes. They didn't move.

"We better leave so they can go," Henry said.

Rachel wanted to watch, so they ran to the crossing rocks and then made their way stealthily upstream on the opposite side of the animal hospital.

"Look there," Rachel whispered. The foxes had scampered to the water's edge and were drinking. Then one darted toward the brush and another one followed, and then the third one.

"Think they'll make it?" Henry asked.

Rachel nodded with pride. "They have a better chance than if they'd been left alone without their mother. Let's go."

They wandered back to the house. The day passed slowly as Henry anticipated the next morning when Father would return.

It was just after twilight when they heard cantering hoof-beats on the road. The beats slowed as the rider turned up the lane to the house.

Mother was the first one outside. Henry followed her.

"George?" she called into the growing darkness.

"Mrs. Lankford, it's me, Nathan Hollister," the rider called out.

"Nathan? What's wrong with George?" Panic laced her voice until it was a shrill shriek.

Nathan, who worked at Father's shipyard, dismounted and tied his horse to a post on the porch.

"Can we go inside?" he asked.

Mother walked into the parlor as if she were in a trance. Henry and Nathan Hollister followed. Everyone was standing up: Miss Emma by the fire, Aunt Betsy and Uncle Andrew, who had been sitting on the settee, even the children, who had been playing on the floor.

They all watched in silence as Nathan Hollister crossed over to the fireplace and extended his hands to the warmth.

"I have a message from George. He's ill. He said he has the first sign."

CHAPTER 14
A Ride to Cincinnati

Mother put her hand over her heart and sat down hard in a chair.

"He also said for you to stay in the country," Nathan said. "He has kept his promise, now you are to promise you will stay in the country."

"No," Mother said. "I made no such promise to him."

"I could sure use a cup of coffee before I go back," Nathan said. "In the kitchen?" He looked pointedly at Henry and Louisa.

"Yes, coffee in the kitchen," Mother said.

"Of course," Aunt Betsy agreed. "In the kitchen."

The adults hurriedly left the parlor.

"They don't want us to hear what they're talking about," Rachel whispered to Henry. "As if we're too young to know."

"I'm going to town," Henry whispered. "I've got to go. Now. Remember what Dr. Drake said. Cholera could take a life in six hours. I'm going to Father."

"We'll ride one of Papa's horses."

"You're going, too?" he whispered.

"I know my way in the dark. You don't." In a loud voice she said, "We're going to check on the horse."

She slipped on her shawl, and Henry grabbed his coat. They went out the front door and circled around to the barn. The full moon lit the way.

Rachel slipped the bridle on the mare and led her out of her stall.

"Carry that saddle outside," she said and pointed to one that straddled a wooden railing.

Together they saddled the horse in the moonlight. Rachel climbed in the saddle, and Henry sat in front of her. She guided the horse through the pasture.

"We don't want them to know we're gone yet," she said. "The grass will muffle the mare's steps."

They had gone maybe half a mile before Rachel turned the horse toward the road.

"Hold on. We're going for a ride," Rachel said. She made a clicking sound with her tongue, and the horse took off. She slowed the horse to a walk a couple times, just for rest, then urged her on again. They were in Cincinnati in well under an hour.

The city was quiet. A hush had settled over it since Henry had left almost three weeks ago. It couldn't have been seven o'clock yet, but there were no wagons in the streets. Many homes were in darkness. A few had soft lantern light pouring from a window.

Henry wrinkled his nose at the smell of burning tar. He'd forgotten some people had used that old preventative method before he'd left town. He wondered if it did anything but make the air stink.

Rachel slowed the horse. It made a clomping sound on the pavement that echoed in the ghostly city. A city of the dead.

"Hurry," Henry said, and Rachel clicked her tongue again.

"Where are we going?"

He didn't know. Father could be at the hospital or at the pesthouse or at home.

"We're close to the hospital. Let's go there first." Father had said he would consult Dr. Drake at the first sign, and the doctor would probably be at the hospital.

Henry slid off the horse once they stopped in front of the hospital and ran inside, while Rachel tied up the horse and wiped it down.

"Sister," he said to the first person he saw, a nun who was scurrying down a narrow hall carrying a bucket. "I'm looking for my father, George Lankford. Is he here?"

"George Lankford," she repeated in a tired voice. "Yes, he was here, but now he's gone."

Henry leaned on the wall to steady himself. He was too late.

"Dr. Drake took him home," Sister continued. "We have no empty beds."

"He's alive?" Henry said in a shaky voice.

"Oh, what have I done?" she said and reached out to Henry. "I meant he was gone from here, not gone from this earth. He's at his home."

"Thank you," Henry called over his shoulder. He walked as fast as his shaky legs could carry him to the entrance, where he met Rachel climbing the steps. "He's at home."

She turned around and ran for the mare. "Is he all right?" she asked once they were on the horse again.

"I don't know." He told her everything the nurse had said.

It seemed a lifetime, but only a few minutes passed before they were on Henry's street. A horse and buggy were tied up in front of the house, and a light glowed from the parlor window.

Henry jumped from the horse and raced to the house. He threw open the front door. No one was in the front room, but a lantern sat on a parlor table. "Father?" he said in a low voice. He walked hesitantly toward the bedroom, afraid of what he might find.

"Henry? Is that you?" He recognized Dr. Drake's voice before the doctor stepped out of the bedroom.

"How's Father?"

"He's got cholera, but I think he's getting treatment in time. I'm just taking leeches off him now. Then I've got to get back to the hospital. You can take over here." He turned and walked back into the bedroom, and Henry followed him.

Father lay in the bed, a pale figure against the white bedding. He wasn't blue. That was a good sign.

"Father!" Henry rushed to his side and leaned over and hugged him.

"Henry. My message was that you were not to come to town," Father said in a weak voice. "Where's your mother?"

"She's at Rachel's. She doesn't know we came."

"Who's with you?"

"Rachel. We'll take care of you."

"Good," Dr. Drake said. "Come in the parlor, and I'll give you instructions."

"I'll be right back, Father." Henry once again followed the doctor.

Rachel stood in the parlor, looking uncertain.

"Good evening, Rachel," Dr. Drake said. "I'm glad you've come, because I need to go, and I couldn't leave Henry's father unattended. I'm giving him massive doses of laudanum, so he's sedated while the calomel works." As he spoke, he wrote down instructions on paper he pulled from his pocket. "He may vomit again, but I hope we've stopped that. Rub his skin continually with this powdered chalk. I'm all out of mercury ointment," he added, almost to himself.

"We can do that," Henry said confidently.

"Here are the leeches for bleeding him again. It's all on this paper. Follow the instructions, and I'll check on him again tomorrow." He turned to leave, then turned back. "You'll do just fine," he said.

"Well, let's get to work," Henry said once the doctor had gone. "I'll start the rubbing."

"I'll unsaddle the horse. I waited," she said uncertainly. "I didn't know what we'd find."

So she'd thought they might be making the dark journey back to the farm to tell Mother the bad news.

"I know. Thank God he's doing all right."

"Yes. Thank God," she said. "Henry, you were more scared yesterday than you are today when your father has cholera."

Henry thought about that for a moment. "You're right. Yesterday my fears were overpowering. But once I asked God to take my fear, I could handle what was making me fearful in the beginning. Odd."

"Maybe not so odd," she said and headed outside.

Henry busied himself in the sickroom, giving his father water and rubbing his skin with the chalking substance to keep him warm. He wouldn't let Father's skin turn blue.

The laudanum was working its wonders, sedating Father so he didn't feel the intense stomach cramps that Henry knew were one of the symptoms.

"What do you want me to do?" Rachel asked from the doorway.

"Help me get the medicines lined up and write down the times for giving them." He handed her the instructions Dr. Drake had written. "Then you can sleep for a while. We'll trade off sleeping and rubbing Father's skin."

They got everything lined out, and Rachel went to the other room to sleep. Henry worked until he felt drowsy. Then he woke her up. He had just sat in the chair by the bed when the sound of horses and a wagon outside arrested his attention. A moment later Mother and Uncle Andrew burst into the house.

"George," Mother said and knelt beside the bed. She took Father's hand and raised it to her lips.

"I told you not to come," he murmured.

"I had to come get your disobedient son," she said and gave Henry one of those looks that said she would deal with him later. "We're taking you to the country. I spoke with Dr. Drake at the hospital, and he says we can move you. As soon as he sees you in the morning, we'll go."

They took turns with Father in the night, giving him medicine, placing the leeches on him, taking them off, and rubbing his skin. By morning he seemed better.

It was midmorning before Dr. Drake returned. He gave Father more medicine and said they were doing a splendid job. "I wish all my patients had this many nurses."

Henry walked with the doctor out to his rig.

"I've kept a log of the temperatures and the clouds and the wind. I don't see how any of them caused the cholera to breed. Should I keep writing them down?"

"Hmmm. Sometimes, Henry, we prove something by disproving what we thought we could prove. Keep recording your data. When life gets back to normal, we'll look for patterns or abnormalities. You're going to make a fine doctor. I wish you were one now. I could use the help." He climbed up in his buggy. "Take care of your father. His recovery may be slow, but I think he'll make it."

"Thank you," Henry called after him.

There was much to be done. Uncle Andrew had gone to Nathan Hollister's to discuss running the shipyard in Father's absence. Rachel and Henry made a bed of heavy quilts in the back of the wagon. When Uncle Andrew returned, they heated bricks in the fireplace and put them in the bed to keep it warm while Mother helped Father put on clean clothes.

When everything was ready, they all carried him to the bed in the wagon and covered him with more heavy quilts. Mother climbed onboard and drove the team while Rachel and Henry sat in the back with Father. They left Uncle Andrew building a fire to burn the bed linen and clothes Father had worn when he got sick. Once the fire had burned out, Uncle Andrew would ride the mare back to the farm.

As they rode out of town, Henry rubbed Father's face, the only part of his skin visible because he was cocooned in quilts. In the distance, Henry heard church bells.

He had forgotten it was Sunday. He raised his eyes to the heavens and said a fervent prayer of thanks.

CHAPTER 15

Safe at Last

The trip back to the farm took much longer than the trip in
the darkness the night before. Henry worried about his father
being cold, but Mother said he should be okay. He was probably sweating under all the heavy quilts. Father didn't say
much, but he mumbled a couple times that he was all right.
His eyes remained shut the entire trip.

Uncle Andrew caught up with them before they were
halfway home.

"I'll ride ahead and have Betsy fix a place for George,"
he said.

"We should isolate him," Mother said.

"It's not contagious," Henry said. "He'll be all right with
us."

"Just the same, we'll isolate him," Mother said in a firm
voice.

By the time Mother turned the wagon into Rachel's lane, Henry could see that Aunt Betsy had settled on the smoke-house as a quarantine place for Father. She and Miss Emma were out there with pails in their hands.

Louisa ran for the wagon. "We've carried all the meat to another shed," she said. "Uncle Andrew's started a fire, and we're moving a bed." She climbed up in the wagon and leaned over Father and kissed him. "I love you, Father." A tear fell on her cheek.

"He's going to be all right," Henry said and patted his sister on the back. He hadn't realized that Louisa had felt all the fear that he had.

"The room's not quite ready," Aunt Betsy said. "Are you okay in the wagon for a while, George?" She had climbed up on a wheel to peer down at Father because there was no more room in the wagon bed.

"The sunshine feels good on my face," Father said. "I'm all right."

"Henry, heat up the bricks," Mother said.

He rummaged around until he located the bricks under the covers, disturbing Father as little as he could. Rachel helped carry them to the fireplace and back to the wagon when they were hot.

"I could stay out here," Father said. "This feels good."

"It won't feel good tonight when there's a frost," Mother said.

By the time they moved Father into the smokehouse, it had been transformed into a bedroom. Henry recognized a parlor table and the bed Mother and Louisa had been sleeping in. Two chairs from the front room were in there, too, and the place still had a smell of the lye soap that Aunt Betsy had used to clean it. A fire burned brightly in the crude fireplace that was used to smoke meat.

Aunt Betsy fixed a schedule so that someone was nursing Father at every minute, night and day. Soon everything had calmed down, and Miss Emma was taking her turn with Father.

"I'm going down to the creek," Rachel said, her hand on the kitchen doorknob. "You coming, Henry?" They had just finished a very late noon meal. Henry got up from his chair to fetch his coat.

"I sent Calvin down this morning to look after your animals," Aunt Betsy said.

Rachel gasped. "You know about my animals?" Her eyes were as big as a deer's.

Uncle Andrew chuckled. "Do you think something can happen on my land that I wouldn't know about?"

"We were hoping you'd tell us what you were doing," Aunt Betsy said.

"I didn't think you'd understand," Rachel said.

"Understand what?" Aunt Betsy asked. She moved around the kitchen table and put her hand on Rachel's shoulder.

"That I like taking care of animals. I want to be an animal doctor." Rachel looked down at the floor. "Ever heard of a girl wanting to do that?"

"I'll admit it's not common," Aunt Betsy said. "But it's uncommon for a girl to play a violin, and I wanted to do that, so I did. If you want to do something bad enough, you can find a way."

Rachel hugged her mother. "I will find a way."

"Good," Uncle Andrew said. "I could use some help with the farm animals. Maybe you ought to start studying about cattle and horses and pigs instead of foxes that raid our chicken coop."

Rachel laughed out loud, and Henry could hear both joy and relief in her voice.

"Maybe you should talk to Slim Watkins," Uncle Andrew said. "Folks call on him when they need help with sick animals."

Rachel's smile was a mile wide. "I'll do that," she said.

Henry shrugged into his coat and joined Rachel at the door.

"Can you imagine?" Rachel said once they were outside. "They want me to be an animal doctor."

"Since you like the country so much, taking care of farm animals seems like the thing you ought to do," Henry said.

"And since you like the city so much, taking care of sick people at a hospital is what you should do," Rachel said.

With those words, Henry sensed an unspoken bond. He would never again think that city ways were better than country ways. There were good things and bad things about both places.

Henry and Rachel ran down to the creek and measured the water, and Henry jotted down his other observations. The injured rabbit was munching on some hay that Calvin had given it.

When they returned to the house, Mother was taking her turn with Father, and Miss Emma sat at the kitchen table.

"How's Father?" Henry asked. His turn to nurse him was next.

"He's going to be fine," Miss Emma said. "He doesn't look at all like Hannah did. He's getting pink color in his face. He's going to be fine."

Henry said a silent thank-you to God. He'd been doing that on and off all day, but he couldn't say it enough to express the relief he felt, the burden lifted.

Miss Emma's prediction was right. A week later Father insisted that he be allowed up and around. Each day he grew stronger, and within a month he proclaimed himself to be better than before his bout with cholera.

Uncle Andrew started going back into Cincinnati on market days. As winter moved in, the cholera lessened its hold on the town. Six weeks later, in mid-December, Miss Emma, Henry, Louisa, Mother, and Father packed their belongings on the wagon.

"Betsy, Andrew, I can't thank you enough for letting my family rely on you," Father said.

"Oh, George, you'd have done the same for us," Aunt Betsy said.

Henry stood to the side with Rachel. "I'll miss the creek and the animals," he said.

"Then come back sometime," she said. "I'll see you in town on Saturday market day, and we'll go talk to Dr. Drake."

"See you then," Henry said and climbed up on the wagon bed.

Father hollered giddyap to the horses, and the family headed back to Cincinnati and home.

Good News for Readers

There's more! The American Adventure continues with *Riot in the Night*. Louisa and Henry Lankford don't like the way black people in Cincinnati are being treated, but they aren't sure what they can do to help. When James Birney, one of the leaders of the movement to end slavery, starts printing a newspaper in Cincinnati, things get violent. Mobs roam the streets at night, looking for Mr. Birney and setting fires. Louisa learns that her friends Mrs. Jackson and Sarah are in danger. Will she and Henry be able to warn them before the mob gets to their home, or will they be too late?